UNEXPECTED RIDE

Other Books in this Series

Rough Ride
Slow Ride
Wild Ride
Long Ride

UNEXPECTED RIDE

*RIDING WITH HONOR SERIES
BOOK 5*

Rebecca M. Avery

This is an original publication of Rebecca M. Avery

This is a work of fiction. Names, characters, places and incidents either are the product of the author's imagination or are being used fictitiously, and any resemblance to actual persons, living or dead, business establishments, events or locales is entirely coincidental.

Copyright © 2013
Rebecca M. Avery

Cover Design by George Guignet (Miserable George)
miserableg@mindspring.com

All Rights Reserved
No part of this book may be reproduced or distributed in any printed or electronic form without permission.

Library of Congress Catalog

ISBN- 978-1492188315

UNEXPECTED RIDE

Rebecca M. Avery

To Kevin whose unexpected and impressive plot development skills made this book possible and to Michelle who is doing a fine job with the hand life dealt her. Both of you should be proud of yourselves.

Chapter One

"I just think it would be better if you stayed at my place... at least for a couple of days until you aren't on the pain medication anymore. Then, if you want to stay at Becca's beach house, I can just come by and check on you a couple of times a week instead," Carla Johnson said to the man sitting on the edge of the hospital bed in a gown that showed more than it covered.

Those silly examination gowns swam on her and often could wrap around her almost twice. On him it looked like an oversized t-shirt and showcased his muscular legs. The really sad part was he looked good even in a hospital gown with his blond hair, which unlike hers, didn't appear to have even a single strand of grey and hazel eyes that sometimes looked green, sometimes brown and sometimes even red. The gunshot wound to his shoulder that required heavy bandages and a sling to keep his arm from pulling on the stitches only added to the air of danger that surrounded him.

Those unique colored eyes followed her around the room wherever she went. She began organizing his clothes into a bag along with the paperwork regarding the proper care of his surgical wound and the sling on his arm. His prescriptions were mixed in with other papers outlining his follow up visit at the doctor's office and the first two outpatient physical therapy appointments that were already scheduled.

"Becca said you were preparing for Thanksgiving and doing stuff for Chuck's birthday, so I'm sure you have better things to do than babysit me," Detective Greg Sanders replied, clearly frustrated. "Why don't you give me a minute to get dressed and we'll discuss this in the car. I am more than ready to get out of here and find some real food."

Standing up he was more than a half a head taller than her. As he straightened to his full height he wobbled slightly and Carla rushed over to where he stood. He shook his head as though trying to clear the fog from the painkillers and antibiotics he had taken with his breakfast. Once he had his bearings, he looked down at where she stood reaching her free hand out to him as if she could actually keep him from falling down with one hand and then he smiled. His lips and smile were the first things she'd noticed about him.

Carla had met Greg a few months ago when her father, Judge Nathan Patterson, brought him and his sister, Becca Waters, to the house for a meeting. The gathering was regarding Chuck Reynolds, who was performing his court ordered community service requirements by helping Carla with her household. Chuck was on probation and Becca was the attorney representing him.

Chuck's community service just happened to have been ordered by Carla's father. Chuck helped Carla with her two sons every week night and sometimes on weekends too. The young man had very quickly made a place for himself in Carla's family as though he were one of her kids as well.

Even with the seriousness of the circumstances that brought Greg and Becca to her home that day, she had immediately been distracted by Greg's mouth and perfect smile. She'd noticed it every time after their initial introduction and today was no exception.

"You asked me to help you out while you recovered and I have the spare room at my house all freshened up for you. You may find that not having the full use of your dominate hand and arm is a little harder to deal with than you think," she said after adjusting all the items she was carrying in order to maintain one free hand to open doors with. "I'll just run this stuff out to my car which is in the little side lot for patient pickup. Then I'll come back in to get the flowers and balloons and walk down with you."

Greg's beautiful mouth smiled even wider upon realizing that her words were spoken directly to his lips and perfect teeth since she couldn't look at anything else. Glancing up at him she quickly backed away from the sexy twinkle flickering in his eyes that she found looking back at her. Then turning away from him she walked out of the room. *She could do this...* help Greg Sanders out for a few weeks until he was back on his feet so to speak. It was the least she could do to try and repay his sister, Becca, who had done so much for Chuck.

Most of Carla's friends thought that the death of her husband, Douglas, almost a year ago had done something to her mental state. In all reality she thanked God for all the changes in her life over this past year. If she had been left *alone* to mourn Doug's passing when it first happened, she might have taken the same path that her daughter, Meredith, had gone down with self-pity and depression.

Instead, by the time Carla had looked up from making Doug's funeral arrangements, filing all the necessary documents with the county, working with the attorney and insurance company regarding the accident, helping the boys cope with the loss of their father, and nursing Meredith back to health, several months had passed. Her two sons, Matt and Ben, were able to grieve for their father but there hadn't been time for Carla to really feel the loss.

After dealing with all the legal matters for both the accident and Doug's death, her focus had shifted to helping Meredith deal with her guilt over the accident. Meredith's emotional downward spiral had been almost more than Carla could bear to watch. Just when she had thought the accident claimed not only her husband but her daughter too, along came one tattooed gangster named Chuck Reynolds, as a direct answer to her prayers for help. The whole neighborhood might think she was crazy for opening her home to the young man and allowing him to care for Matt and Ben, but Carla recognized an angel when she saw one… even if that angel looked like a thug on the outside.

Carla smiled while thinking of her new makeshift family as she organized all of Greg's things in the trunk of her car. She kept his prescriptions with her and put them in her purse so that she could stop at the pharmacy on her way home. She would never have pictured her daughter dating someone like Chuck prior to the accident, but the young man had been Meredith's lifeline in the storm.

Chuck and Meredith falling in love had been so different than Carla's own experience with romance, she had wondered if it happened too fast for them, but watching them together over the past few months had quickly put her fears to rest. Though their love was different than what Carla had shared with her late husband, it was meant to be and she had no doubt they would make it.

Douglas Johnson had come into Carla's life before Meredith's first birthday and his take charge, organized personality had been just what she had needed to heal after her failed relationship and engagement to Meredith's biological father. It had taken until Meredith was nearly three years old before she and Doug had actually married. Her late husband had adopted Meredith legally not long after that and had been more of a father to Meredith than Carla could have ever hoped for. Nothing would replace him... *ever*. Not a day went by that Carla didn't think of his kind eyes and what a wonderful man he was. *She missed him.*

Feeling herself tear up, she knew she still didn't have time to lose herself in the pain that simmered just beneath the surface like a warm pot of soup, waiting for her to acknowledge it. Instead she set it on the back burner yet again and headed back inside the hospital.

Someday it would be her turn... her turn to grieve, her turn to face her uncertain future, her turn to start a new life, but today wasn't that day. Today was about helping out one of the many new friends she had made since Chuck had come into their lives.

She stopped mid-step upon entering Greg's room, startled at seeing the expanse of naked, muscular chest displaying a thin patch of blond hair trailing a path down the center and disappearing into a pair of jeans that were zipped but unbuttoned. Doug had been a wonderful husband and father but right now it was a little hard to keep his memory in the front of her mind because she could not remember Doug ever looking like what was on display at the moment. Even the momentary feeling of guilt for looking wasn't enough to make her look away.

Greg was almost the same height as Doug had been but where Doug had been on the chunky side, which he then allowed to settle around his belly as middle age happened, Greg looked like working out was his other full time job. *She should be ashamed for scoping out a man that wasn't her husband... but just look at him!*

"Can you help with this?" Greg asked with a high level of anxiety and frustration in his voice.

"Yea... sure," she replied.

Her eyes again followed the thin line of hair down his flat, sculpted stomach to rest on the button of his jeans that he held loosely in his left hand. *Focus.* Walking over to him, she stopped in front of him and he let go of the button. He wasn't the only one who would have to adjust to all the things he couldn't do for himself without the use of his dominate hand and arm. Never in her life had buttoning a pair of jeans felt so intimate.

She slowly reached out and grasped the button and the opposing side of his jeans and pulled the two sides closer to each other which only succeeded in rubbing the backs of her fingers against the nicest looking abs she'd seen up close and personal like this... *ever*. His sharp intake of breath brought her eyes up to his handsome face only to settle on his full lips. *On top of his obvious reaction to her touch, why did he have to be so handsome?*

After getting his pants buttoned she reached for his shirt at the same time he did and their hands met.

She released her hold on the material while stepping back to give him room and went to gather up the balloons and flowers to put them on a cart one of the nurses had brought in to the room. Once everything was situated, she turned back to find him sitting on the edge of the bed again with his uninjured arm through one sleeve and a perplexed look on his face while the other sleeve was halfway over his sling. Walking back over to him, she adjusted the sleeve guiding it up and over the sling, then settled it in place before bunching up the shirt to make it easier to slip over his head and was suddenly stopped by the frown on his face.

"I can do the rest," he said gruffly.

Uncomfortable with just how aware of him she was from simply buttoning his pants and standing close to him, she released his shirt and again stepped away from him. She turned her back to him but could still hear him wrestling with the shirt. After a few moments she glanced back over her shoulder and found he had managed to cover up the only other part of him that drew her eyes as much as his mouth did.

Making her way to the chair in the corner of the room she sat down and watched as he managed to separate his socks and finally get one on. She was surprised at how much she wanted to just go and take over for him since there was no way he would be able to tie his own shoes.

"Would you like some help with your shoes?" she asked after he finally managed to get his other sock on as well.

"No... I've got it," he replied tersely.

Fine. As much as it was killing her to watch him struggle, much like with her kids... Meredith, Matt or Ben and sometimes even Chuck, she would let him either figure it out on his own or wait for him to ask for help. Stubbornness could sometimes be a benefit... at least it had been for Meredith when she'd finally decided to take back control of her own life after the accident. Perhaps the same would be true for Greg Sanders. Somehow watching him struggle was even harder than watching the kids since this wasn't a learning experience for him... this was just a waste of time... and all because he wouldn't allow her to help.

"Are you sure... I don't mind," she offered again after what felt like an hour passed while he tried to pull his heavy boots on with his left hand.

Sighing heavily he said, "Since you are in such a hurry... *sure*... please put my shoes on for me." The sarcasm in his voice brought out a level of childishness in her she hadn't experienced in more than decade.

Glancing at her watch she said, "It's just that the pharmacy closes at nine and we need to get your prescriptions filled yet."

She watched his amazing eyes glance at the clock hanging on the wall which showed it wasn't even one o'clock yet. Then that smile spread across his beautiful mouth and she could swear he blushed. As if he needed any more physical attributes to make him attractive... blushing only *added* to his sex appeal. *Concentrate.* His eyes looked green when her gaze made it from those lips back up to return his stare. Now she was blushing... *good grief.*

"I'm sorry... I just hate this," he said, his grin widening as she stood and approached where he sat. To emphasize his point he tried to raise his injured arm and the look of pain that crossed his handsome face had her forgiving him in the time it took to reach his side.

"Are you okay?" she asked, stopping directly in front of him.

"Yea... I think that hurt as bad as getting shot did," he replied.

The idea that police officers and firemen put their lives on the line every day had just been a phrase she'd heard... a statement she was familiar with... but until she met Greg it didn't really hold any meaning for her. *He could have died!* Instead, his gunshot wound had been repaired with surgery and his mobility would return with the help of a physical therapist.

To Carla the idea of being shot brought about a breathtaking fear. For Greg Sanders it was all part of the job and the wound was currently keeping him from doing his.

She knelt down in front of him and held open one of his large boots while he slipped his foot inside after grasping her shoulder for balance and leverage. She managed to tie up the boot and then put the other one on and tie it as well. After finishing she looked up at him and found him watching her while biting on one side of his full lower lip.

His thoughts were mirrored in his eyes and she found herself lost in in his gaze for a moment until he finally cleared his throat and looked away from her. It had been a while since she'd been with a man, more than just the year since Doug's death, but Greg's hand on her shoulder and his uneven breathing left little doubt what he had been imagining.

Making every effort not to look at him, she got up from where she'd knelt to put his shoes on and grabbing her purse she went to the cart and waited with her back to him. Standing there listening to the awkward silence that filled the room, she tried to will the burning in her cheeks back into check with little to no success. After several moments she decided that she could go on and push the cart down to the car to unload it. He didn't need help walking and could make his way to the car on his own. He didn't need her for that.

Pushing the cart towards the door, her attempts at escape were thwarted when he said, "Wait, I can get the cart."

Great... now getting down to the car would take twice as long as need be... much like putting on his clothes had. Unwilling and quite honestly unable to talk to him at the moment, let alone argue, she let go of the cart. Stepping to the door of the room, she held it open.

A clear invitation for him to take his best shot at guiding the cart out of the room. That offer was heavily regretted minutes later when he finally managed to steer the cart through the doorway with his left hand.

By the time they made it down to the lobby she had no patience left. Placing her hand on the handle of the cart she said, "You are on narcotics for pain which means that if I let you roll this thing across the parking lot then essentially I am allowing you to drive under the influence... correct?"

She hadn't realized how close she was standing to him until he turned his head to the side to look at her. Whatever argument he had, died before ever being spoken when her eyes went straight to his mouth. For once she could respect why a man would talk to a woman while staring at her breasts because his lips had that same effect on her and no amount of shame kept her from looking at them.

The only thing that broke her gaze was catching his hand motioning for her to take over. As much as she wanted to push the cart to her car as quickly as possible just to get away from him, it would do no good since within a few minutes he would be in the vehicle with her. There was no escape from his handsome face, the wicked sensations just being near him brought out in her and definitely no way to keep from staring at his mouth.

Getting him in the car turned out to be yet another lesson on those things that were harder for him to do for himself now. After getting in the front passenger seat, instead of waiting for her to close the door for him after unloading the items from the cart into the car, he reached across his body and tried closing the door with his left hand.

This simply jostled his injured arm before the door bumped it which resulted in a stream of cuss words and a couple of sharp breaths on his part. Rather than saving him from his own stupidity, she finished unloading the cart and then walked over to his side of the car. Catching his gaze to ensure he knew what she was about to do, she closed the door for him. *No pain this time.* She nearly laughed out loud when she noticed Greg rolling his eyes after he thought she wasn't looking.

The trip to the pharmacy was much the same. Try as she might not to get frustrated at his unwillingness to ask for help as well as his refusal to *accept* help, she was ready for a shot of something out of the liquor cabinet by the time they made it back to the house. Thankfully, Chuck had made lunch for the boys while Meredith went to a baby shower for Lilly Jackson.

Lilly was actually a friend of both Carla and Meredith. She and her husband Bobby owned a motorcycle repair shop where both Chuck and Meredith were working at the moment. Carla had wanted to go to the baby shower as well but not wanting Greg's sister, Becca, to miss it for having to pick him up from the hospital, Carla had just sent her gift with Meredith instead. Becca had done some legal work for Lilly and Bobby as well. Carla knew how much Becca wanted to go so she had offered to pick Greg up since she would be helping him out for a while anyways.

After getting Greg situated at the breakfast bar in the kitchen and then unloading the car, Carla asked, "Would you like a salad for lunch?" His frown told her he had hopes for something more substantial.

Laughing, she said, "Or at least something light for lunch since I was thinking of grilling this evening."

"Yea, salad is fine," he replied sitting down on one of the barstools.

As she began pulling out fresh vegetables to cut up for the salad, Chuck entered the kitchen and said, "The boys ate a good lunch and Nathan said he would pick them up around three this afternoon." Then, after a brief pause in which he studied her closely, he said, "Are you going to be okay here by yourself until we get back?"

For having grown up without anything even remotely resembling a family, Chuck's perceptiveness was second to none. Knowing that tomorrow would have been her and Doug's anniversary, Chuck was clearly torn between taking Meredith to the beach that Doug always took her to and not leaving Carla alone overnight at such a time. The young man stood hesitantly waiting for her response.

"She'll be fine… I'll be here with her since she insists on treating me like an invalid," Greg replied.

Chuck looked between them for a moment before nodding his acknowledgment at Greg. Then he picked up a duffle bag he had brought downstairs, looked at Carla and said, "Call us if you need us, hot stuff."

"I could always just take you back to the hospital," Carla threatened Greg after Chuck left and they were once again alone in the kitchen.

"You don't want to send me back there," Greg replied with a smile. "Then you would just have to continue visiting me there every day in order to boss me around."

"Bossing you around? Is that what they call it these days? I have always referred to it as trying to help," she smiled back as she began chopping up the ingredients for the salad.

"Chuck's awful protective of you isn't he?" Greg asked.

"Becca said much the same thing a while back. I think it's for two reasons. One is that he doesn't want to think of Meredith suffering anymore loss, especially losing *another* parent. The second reason is that he is just now experiencing what it is like to have a family, so he doesn't want anything to ruin that," she replied.

"I understand that but I would think you've spent time alone here before… even since the break-in. He isn't worried because I'm here is he?" he asked as she set his salad down in front of him along with a napkin and a fork.

Carla tried not to think of that horrible day, when Chuck's unfortunate past caught up to him here… *in her home*… where she thought he would be safe. In this case, it was more a matter of her mental state than her physical safety that caused Chuck such concern. Having always been very emotional, Carla was used to it, as were the boys and Meredith, but it somehow bothered Chuck to witness her tears. Knowing that tomorrow would have been their anniversary had put the young man on full alert.

"It's not that… tomorrow is… would have been… my wedding anniversary. Aside from birthdays and holidays that is the worst," she finished softly.

Feeling the sting of tears that were always simmering in the background when she thought of the accident, especially here recently, she swallowed several times trying to rein them in. Once she was able to get it together she sat down at the bar with him and they ate in companionable silence.

When he finished she convinced him to take some pain medicine and then lay down for a while. Then she pulled out a small package of steaks to grill and set them to marinating. She also made a list of those items she still needed to get at the store for Thanksgiving Dinner and for Chuck's birthday both of which she would be hosting the following weekend.

Since Chuck was gone she went ahead and pulled his birthday gifts out of the closet in her bedroom and wrapped them while the boys watched television and waited for their grandfather in the living room. By the time her father picked up the boys for the weekend, she was in need of a nap herself but instead decided to read over the care instructions from the hospital.

Having spent all those months caring for Meredith's injuries, she should be a professional at it by now but for some strange reason she found reading about how to care for wounds and the different types of medications used to treat injuries interesting. The fact that Greg Sanders was the one she would be taking care of only heightened her interest in making sure she was able to do so properly.

"What are you reading?" Greg's voice made her jump since she hadn't known he was even awake let alone that he had come downstairs. She had been so engrossed in the pamphlets from the hospital she'd lost track of time.

"Oh nothing really. Are you hungry? I could go ahead and start dinner," she offered, setting the brochures aside.

"Sure. Can I help?" he asked.

"I'm not sure what you could possibly do one handed but you can keep me company if you'd like," she suggested, getting up from the couch and walking into the kitchen.

He followed her and sat at the bar again as she pulled a pineapple out of the refrigerator and began cutting it so she could grill it.

"Do you mind if I ask you a personal question?" he asked after she managed to cut the prickly outer shell off of the pineapple.

Swallowing hard she said, "Sure, go ahead."

What could he possibly want to know? He was such a handsome man that he probably had his pick of women or possibly a serious girlfriend back in New York. Though it was doubtful he was in a relationship because if he were the woman would have come down here to Florida in order to be with him when he was injured. *Right?*

"What was your husband like and how long were you married?" he asked as she cored the pineapple and then began to cut it into thick slices.

Of all the things he could have asked her, that was the one thing she least expected. Almost no one asked her about Doug both right after the accident or even now that some time had passed. Perhaps they didn't ask out of fear that trudging up memories of the accident and of losing the man she loved would be too painful for her to talk about.

Or maybe they were just unsure what to say. Either way, it kept people from asking. Now that someone had finally asked her about Doug, what could she say? What did Greg really want to know? Did he want her good memories of being with Doug, the bad part of losing him, the funny things he used to say or maybe the guilt she felt that she'd not been the one who had went out in the storm to pick up Meredith that night.

This time when the tears burned in her eyes there was no turning them down or even off completely. Instead she could feel them sliding silently down her cheeks. All these months... a year in fact... she had let her grief simmer and it chose now to boil over? Fighting the emotions only succeeded in making her throat burn as well.

She both heard and felt him approach where she stood until one thick muscled left arm forced her to set the knife down she still held. Then it wrapped around her shoulders from behind and cupped the side of her face. He awkwardly pulled at her until she gave in and turned into his embrace. He kept his injured arm turned away from her to avoid accidentally bumping it as he had earlier in the car but he held her none the less.

Holding her against him she could not help but take in the scent of his aftershave but beyond how good he smelled and his devastating smile was something she desired even more. *Comfort.*

There had been so many friends that she and Doug had known over the course of their marriage that had shown up for his funeral. Their kind words and hugs had tried to offer condolences. Even the group of bikers she had come to know vicariously through Chuck often tried to offer comfort. This man who rarely actually spoke to her and only had one shoulder to offer at the moment was whose arms she found around her now that the flood gates were finally open.

"I guess that answers my real question," he whispered into her hair. "I'm sorry for your loss and though it's nothing in comparison to what you've already done for me over this past week, I hope that I can be here for you in return."

Chapter Two

Having watched Carla fall apart in his arms was an experience Greg hoped never to have to repeat for as long as he lived. That was the only reason he was still using the guest room in her home instead of going to stay at the beach house. It had been nearly two weeks since the surgery on his shoulder and a full week since he'd been released from the hospital.

His follow up appointment with the surgeon a couple of days ago had resulted in having some of the stitches removed and getting confirmation that the infection that had kept him in the hospital much longer than he would have preferred was gone.

The man who shot him had been arraigned and brought before a grand jury. According to Becca, who was the intended victim, the man had taken a plea deal so a trial wouldn't be necessary. However, Greg was still stuck in Florida until he was well enough to travel back home to New York.

There were a couple more physical therapy sessions coming up but his arm and shoulder still ached horribly. As if that wasn't bad enough the stupid sling that kept his arm at an odd angle did nothing more than annoy him and itch like it was infested with fleas.

He had a doctor's appointment in a little while and was hoping the last remaining stitches and the sling would be things of the past because all he could think about was taking a shower… baths were for women and little kids. The surgeon had advised him to keep his arm in the sling and avoid getting his surgical wound wet, which made showers next to impossible.

As if he could actually shower one handed anyways. His uninjured arm was too useless to do a very good job at even something simple, like washing his hair.

Frustration was his middle name and tomorrow Carla was having half the state over for Thanksgiving dinner and a birthday party for Chuck. She had insisted that Greg at least stay until after the holiday was over before going to stay at his sister's beach house. This meant he should at least attempt to shave since he was starting to resemble something that just came down out of the mountains. And maybe take another stab at shampooing his hair.

After her emotional outburst his first day out of the hospital, he had listened as Carla talked about her late husband and how much she missed him. The following day he had went with her to visit her husband's grave and then that Sunday he went to the cemetery again with Carla, her two boys, Meredith and Chuck.

Seeing the soft hearted woman trying to comfort her children had made Greg want to be there for her even more as she tried to be the rock her children needed as they remembered the life… *and death…* of their father.

Aside from trying to be a friend to Carla since, much to his disappointment, she wasn't really ready for anything else, he had been pretty much useless after getting out of the hospital. His left arm was nothing more than an appendage to make him appear symmetrical.

Besides wiping his own ass and feeding himself with a fork or spoon there wasn't much else it was useful for. Carla knew this but for the most part was patient when he felt the need to at least attempt to do things for himself. This only served to piss him off more since he wasn't just another one of her children she needed to take care of and encourage.

"Sports are good for kids and can *help* their grades, right, Mom?" Carla's oldest son, Matt, said as he entered the kitchen.

"I appreciate your attempts to help your brother, but no football until he starts doing better in school. He needs to be worried about paying attention and doing his assignments when he is supposed to," Carla replied as she gathered up her keys and purse.

"But, Mom, he *loves* football! Maybe if he plays it will use up some of his energy so he *can* pay better attention," Matt argued.

"No... absolutely not... so arguing is pointless. That is the end of this discussion," Carla said and then looking at where Greg sat at the bar she said, "Are you ready to go?"

When he nodded she looked back at Matt and said, "I'll see you when I get back. Behave yourself for your sister and make sure your room is picked up for tomorrow."

Matt huffed out of the kitchen and Greg followed Carla out to her car. Her youngest son Ben was six and a half and in first grade and had talked non-stop for most of the week about playing flag football. He had brought home paperwork from school for Carla to look at during the holiday break for a pee wee league that was forming since Ben was still too young to play for the school.

Unfortunately he'd also brought home a less than favorable report from the teacher about paying attention in class and not talking so much.

Though Greg hadn't been around long enough to actually watch Ben play, even Chuck had expressed that the boy was a natural. Being able to play was one thing but even if he wasn't able to play so well just yet, his size would make up for any lack of skill. At six, Ben was almost the same size as his older brother, Matt, who was nine. Ben was tall for his age and built like he belonged on the defensive line.

As much as Greg shouldn't get involved since it wasn't really any of his business and for the most part they all ignored the fact that he was even there anyways, Matt did have a point.

Greg had also been one of those kids with too much energy and a healthy dose of adrenaline that was often released at the wrong times, so he could relate to Ben. Hell, he had been bored out of his skull most of this past week while he'd been unable to do much, so having to sit still all day at school was probably really hard to do for a six year old boy.

"I don't mean to pry but…" he started to say when she got in the driver's seat after having closed his door.

"Then please don't..." Carla said, obviously frustrated. "I feel like the only one in the whole house who thinks that Ben's behavior and grades are more important than his obsession with football. Even Chuck acts like I am being too harsh on him... but his schoolwork has to come first."

Waving his left hand defensively he said, "Sorry. I just think that Matt has a point. An overactive boy having to sit still and pay attention to things he couldn't care less about is probably even harder if every muscle in his body desperately wants to get up and move. That's all..."

"I understand that but I can't hold him to a lower standard than I expected out of Meredith and Matt... it's not fair to them or to Ben for that matter. I realize he struggles a little more with his school work and is much more active than either of them has ever been, but he may just need to try harder since it doesn't come as easy for him," Carla replied. "He's kind of like bull in a china shop most of the time so I can understand why his teacher has problems with him."

"He's built like one too," Greg mumbled under his breath and then said, "Was your husband a big man?"

As much as he feared she might again break down crying over the husband she clearly loved and missed, she needed to talk about him. That much was obvious. She looked thoughtful for a moment and then smirked slightly.

"Ben definitely has more of his father's build than mine. I think he will end up being bigger than Doug was though... taller *and* bulkier. Doug was about your height but over the years he became... heavy. Ben isn't overweight, he's just really big for his age," Carla smiled at whatever memory or thought was behind the faraway look in her eyes.

He remained quiet about the topic during the remainder of the car ride. As he sat in the waiting room and then in the examination room and then later in another room after getting another set of x-rays taken, he truly could sympathize with Ben's situation. *Sitting still sucked.*

"Would you like a magazine or something to read?" Carla asked him as he once again changed positions in his chair.

"No," he said a little more intensely than he should have.

"Sorry... you are just antsy and I thought maybe you were bored," Carla said, looking at his mouth.

She really needed to stop doing that because staring at his lips just made him want to kiss her with them... maybe use them to make *her* antsy.

Most of the women he dated were what he and the other single guys on the force referred to as holster sniffers... women who chased and slept with cops or tried to marry them. Most of them were considerably younger than him and sometimes not very smart. A few of them had been real lookers. None of them had felt so honest and real... not like Carla. She didn't try to get him to take notice of her which only served to make him more interested.

Carla was a looker too but, rather than lots of curves and makeup paired with tight or skimpy clothes, she was a classic beauty. Large round brown eyes that nearly swallowed a person whole when they looked at you and a pert little nose were the first things Greg noticed about her.

She had light brown hair that was cut really short like a man's haircut, which he normally didn't care for on a woman, but on her it showed her slender neck. Making him want to touch it or kiss it with his mouth that she was always staring at.

"Maybe I need to play a little football or do *something* strenuous… to expend some of my excess energy so *I* can sit still," he said, grinning like an idiot.

Those brown eyes met his gaze quickly when the meaning behind his words sank in. He was a little unprepared when she smiled sadly and then said, "I think I miss that the most… my husband was always teasing me like that."

Not exactly what he wanted to hear… but having done a little detective work by asking people who were closest to Carla… mainly her daughter, Meredith… he knew she really needed to talk about the accident and the effect it had on *her* life. That would not stop him from trying to get her to notice him as a man.

"I wasn't trying to tease you… I was trying to tempt you," he replied.

Her eyes went right back to his lips and hers parted slightly as though inviting him to taste them. He recognized when a woman was turned on, or at least interested, and Carla was one or both. *Success!* He was pretty sure if his shoulder would allow it he might get a penalty for excessive celebration right here in the doctor's office.

Becca had been right when she told him that Carla's disinterest every time he had seen her or talked to her over the past few months was because she hadn't finished grieving for her husband yet. She had said that until Carla actually did or at least started the process, she wouldn't be able to move on. After a weekend of tears and a couple of conversations about her late husband, Carla was actually starting to notice that Greg existed. Did that mean she was working through her grief… or that she might be interested in him? *Or both?*

He wasn't really sure why he had such a feeling of exhilaration over the idea that she not only was aware of him now but had even responded to him a little bit, but he did. Having tried several times to provoke a response from her and waiting much longer for an acknowledgment than he would for most women, it made him a little upset when the doctor chose that moment to enter the room and effectively kill the mood. Carla immediately went back to treating him like another one of her children. *Damn it!*

Maybe because he'd never had children of his own and was clueless on how to be a parent maybe that was why it felt that way. Perhaps it was hard to switch back and forth between parent role and regular adult mode. Thinking about it, Carla treated Meredith and Chuck the same way and they were also adults. Greg was just being sensitive because in an instant his whole life had changed. Almost dying did that for a person… made you start questioning and considering things you'd never paid attention to before… like when a woman stared so intently at your mouth that all you could think about was tasting her with it.

"The arm and shoulder are healing nicely for a man your age. Being healthy, in good shape and active helps the healing process along. I'm willing to remove the rest of the stitches today. However, I do think we need to keep the sling in place for at least another week while you work with the therapist," the doctor said. Upon seeing the look of frustration that Greg knew must be written all over his face, the doctor continued. "The receptionist did express to me how anxious you were to get the sling off today… all three times you called… but quite honestly that gash in your shoulder needs a little more time to heal."

Taking a deep breath to keep from lighting into the man since the frustration he felt had nothing to do with doctor and was in no way his fault, Greg finally said, "What is this going to do regarding getting to go back to work?"

"I've got to be honest with you… it is going to be a little while," the doctor replied. "That is your shooting arm from what I understand, so I do not want to be too hasty in releasing you for active duty. Your arm and shoulder being able to function in a normal capacity could mean the difference between life and death for you or someone else and that I take very seriously, Detective. I'm sorry. Come back in after the holiday and we will take another look and hopefully by then…"

He hated to admit it but the doctor was probably right. Sure he had to be able to shoot with either hand to qualify but in a bad situation most people went for their dominate hand. Feeling the tension in the room and knowing there was nothing more that could be done for his situation that wasn't already being done, he said, "Damn! And I was so looking forward to that shower too."

The doctor chuckled and filled out a prescription for more painkillers that Greg really didn't want. Then they all walked up front to schedule the next appointment. The ride to the pharmacy was quiet and after parking Carla took one look at him and didn't even bother to ask if he wanted to go in with her.

It wasn't her fault either but his job was his *life*. Being single with Becca as his only living relative had meant he worked double shifts often over his career and most holidays too. Honestly, it was all he knew…

He had a few serious relationships over the years, a couple of which made it all the way to the living with each other phase, before the woman figured out he was already married... *to his job.* They promptly called it quits and he just picked up more hours to fill the void they left behind.

Dating a cop or even just sleeping with one was exciting for a moment but the moment passed quickly for a woman left alone while he was out investigating a case. At least he was a little smarter than some of the guys on the force and hadn't married either of the women and had kids with them. Someone who wasn't in law enforcement wasn't as able to relate to the stress of the job.

Being shot and his lengthy stay in the hospital had given him time to reevaluate both of those failed relationships. Carla had visited him every single day... even more than Becca... and he felt pretty sure that neither of the women from his past that he had been committed to would have done that.

He would like to return the favor to Carla but with at least another week, if not more, of being in this ridiculous sling, that wasn't going to happen. Being a cop wasn't just about catching the bad guys... it was also about helping people and right now he couldn't even do that.

Carla studied him for a moment after filling his prescription and coming back out to the car. This time she wasn't looking at his mouth so he didn't even get the satisfaction of a little sexual tension to brighten his mood. He must not just feel like shit but apparently was starting to look like it too because she reached over and brushed his hair back off his forehead with her hand. He was only able to half wash his hair because of the sling and not wanting to risk getting his surgical wound wet and he still wouldn't be able to shave either.

The rest of the evening was a little better at least. After dinner the boys and Chuck joined him in the living room to watch college football while Meredith and Carla began preparing food for the following day. During commercial breaks, Chuck would go to the kitchen and offer to help. Greg was happy for Chuck and Meredith but watching them together made him downright jealous. They were constantly smiling at each other or kissing and touching. He had at least twenty years on them both and had never experienced what they had.

The only respite he got from their disgusting displays of affection was when Carla came in and offered him either a beer or a painkiller. Since he had yet to take one of the pills from the new prescription because they made his tongue feel like there was fuzz on it, he opted to again skip the pill and go for the beer. When he thanked her, this time her gaze went to his lips and he couldn't stop the smile he felt. Maybe he didn't want her to stop staring at his mouth after all. It was sexy as hell to think of all the things that just might be going through her mind when she did that...

When the game ended Chuck helped Meredith pack up some of the food and they went to stay at his apartment. Meredith would cook the food there and bring it back the following day, leaving Carla's oven free for more food. After the boys went upstairs to bed he headed into the kitchen and watched as Carla finished wiping down the countertops of her spacious kitchen. She was always taking care of something or someone... it's who she was and it fascinated him more than he cared to admit.

Unlike the women he was used to... she had yet to ask him for anything in return for all that she was doing for him. She was always the one doing things for other people. *Giving*. Watching her ignore him in favor of finishing her task made him wish his arm and shoulder were better so he could go and run his hands through her hair and press himself against her. Caress her skin or rub his lips along her fragile looking neck or maybe something more *strenuous*. Instead he just watched and waited for her to acknowledge him.

Draping the dishcloth she held across the sink she turned to him and said, "How about I help you bathe, wash your hair and even shave. It may not be as good as a shower but it might make you feel better."

He had just been imagining her mouth parted and his name on her lips while she had been considering how to bathe him. Awkward and sexy at the same time was a new one for him but the blush on her cheeks helped him jump the fence so he was fully on the side of sexy.

"I figure I can run you a bath and you could get in and drape a cloth across… yourself… and then lean back. I can use a cup to rinse your hair and the sink is right next to the tub so I could use it to shave you… *your face*," she quickly clarified. The flush on her cheeks made him want to kiss her even more.

"I considered trying to shave yesterday but with the medications I was nervous I wouldn't be able to tell if I sliced through my jugular," he said. "It makes my tongue feel weird and makes me shake for some reason."

"Why didn't you tell the doctor earlier… he could've maybe prescribed something else," she asked.

"I don't know… but I'm glad I didn't now," he said through his smile.

"I suppose we could just call him after the holidays about a different prescription," she said ignoring his comment completely.

Sighing he said, "I'll go start the water then."

God help him but even with her completely ignoring his attempts to flirt with her he was partially aroused. *What was it about her that made him keep trying to gain her interest?* He needed to start thinking of something else… anything that didn't involve flirting, kissing or touching Carla Johnson. He had *maybe* ten minutes to do so before she would be aware of his mindset.

As he ran water into her oversized bathtub, the anticipation of her touching him… even just to wash his hair made thinking of anything but kissing and flirting with her next to impossible. He chose a hand towel rather than a wash cloth to cover up with before realizing she would have to unsnap his jeans and help him out of the sling anyways.

Maybe this wasn't such a good idea after all. Being helpless as a babe was pretty humiliating but having an erection from thoughts of a woman who mostly ignored him was even more so. *Save his pride or sacrifice it for cleanliness?*

Her soft knock on the door made his mind up for him when she then entered carrying a hand towel, a man's razor and shaving cream. She set the items on the vanity and then approached him and helped him out of his shirt, her thin fingers igniting a sensual torment each place they touched. She helped him get his arm out of the sling as well. Then she gently draped the towel around his shoulders.

He couldn't help but stare at her face while she concentrated on her tasks. Being this close to him, she was even prettier than normal. Chemistry flowed between them that took his breath away and the air around them changed. *Could she not feel that or was she just that good at ignoring it... him?* Just when he began to think she was either oblivious to the tension between them or that it was all in his head, her gaze met his and she slowly reached down and unbuttoned his pants. *Not good.*

"Sorry…" he said by way of an explanation as she maneuvered the zipper of his jeans down, relieving the pressure of the best erection he'd had in a while. *Why was she still staring at him?* When her gaze finally drifted to his mouth, he went back to wishing she wouldn't do that because it made this whole thing even worse for him.

"Let me know when you're all situated and I'll come back in," she said softly and then turned and left, closing the bathroom door behind her.

He maneuvered out of the rest of his clothes and managed to get in the bathtub and cover himself. He sat there for several minutes trying to force his body back into submission. Finally giving up on salvaging any of his dignity he cleared his throat and managed to croak out, "Okay."

She came back in and closed the door and walked over to where he sat with a now wet hand towel covering the elephant in the room. Sitting down on the edge of the tub she scanned his body from head to toe and for the first time in his whole life he felt what some of the people he busted must feel.
Embarrassment, shame and nervousness over being caught.

"I think I should shave you first and then we can work on shampooing your hair," she said as though ignoring his reaction to her meant it didn't happen... or didn't still exist.

She grabbed the razor off the vanity and attached a new blade to it and then set it aside. Using a washcloth she wet his cheeks and then began applying shaving cream to his face. Watching her expressions as she focused so intently on what she was doing helped ease the awkwardness of his situation.

The feel of her hands on his face was wonderful and instead of fearing she would cut him he relaxed and watched as she slowly shaved him. Occasionally she would look him in the eye and smile. Once she even said, "Close your eyes or something... don't watch me... it makes me... nervous."

This was the first time since being shot he was actually enjoying being helpless and having someone else take care of him. By the time she finished and washed his face off with a washcloth the sexual tension between them had returned along with his perpetual erection. He had thought she was pretty the first time he'd met her and she had drawn his attention then with her kindness and giving spirit.

Now along with being attracted to her as a person, there was a growing desire to make love to her. The feeling was different than anything he could remember experiencing before. He had experienced passion before but this was a need he couldn't explain. Instead he watched as she gently eased his head back against the edge of the tub and slowly poured water over his hair. This must be what heaven was like because it felt so good he could only close his eyes.

As she lathered up his hair and scrubbed his scalp with her fingertips he could no longer hold in the moan that had been lodged in his throat since she started this whole process. When she quit he opened his eyes and found her face close to his and instinct had him moving toward her until she abruptly moved back and grabbed the cup to begin slowly rinsing his hair. Damn! *Too far too fast.* She was grieving still and he needed to remember that.

She shampooed his hair a second time and after rinsing it she said, "I'll go grab your sweatpants. I washed them earlier."

He felt her leave... it was a strange feeling to be able to feel another person's presence that way but he could sense Carla. Shaking away his weird thoughts, he washed and was surprised just how much better he did feel both physical and mentally. She came back in and put his clothes on the vanity and turned again to leave.

"Carla?" he said.

She turned back to him and he said, "Thank you for that... it was... wonderful."

Her eyes went straight to his mouth and if not for injuries which slowed him down he would have been out of the bathtub and kissing her in an instant. Instead he could only sit there and let her look her fill. His last serious girlfriend had told him a few times that his lips were really sexy for a man but the way Carla said it… with nothing but her eyes… was unexpected and slowly making him crazy for her.

"Yes it was," she replied so softly he almost missed it. Then she was gone, closing the door behind her.

Chapter Three

The following morning when the phone rang, Carla answered it without looking at the caller ID expecting it to be Meredith with questions on what temperature setting to use for one of the covered dishes she was responsible for baking.

"It looks like our little girl made a good choice for a groom. I must say when I first picked up the paper and seen this guy's picture I thought perhaps with losing Doug and everything, your judgment was slipping," a familiar male voice stated when she answered.

As if she didn't have enough things on her plate, why did he have to crawl back out from beneath the rock he had been hiding under now? The sad part was after all these years… she still recognized his voice. *Jarrod Tompkins.* To think at one point in her life she'd thought herself in love with the bastard… was simply unconscionable now.

"Yes, *my* daughter chose well. Why are you calling me and what do you want?" she asked, attempting to keep the fear and contempt she felt out of her voice.

What she should have asked was what… or how much… it would take to get him to go away *again*… at least for another couple of decades. A small sliver of fear swept up her spine as her mind contemplated any and every reason he could possibly have for calling her now. Had he also called her father… or God forbid… Meredith?

"I think it is time that I actually meet her. I do not in any way proclaim to be Father of the Year but this isn't about me. It's about Meredith. She deserves to know the truth and be given an opportunity to make her own decisions about me. Perhaps she will find it in her heart to forgive me for not being a better person and for my past mistakes. Maybe she will *want* to get to know me. Seeing her with this Charles Reynolds guy she's pictured with, makes me think that maybe she's more forgiving than you and your father ever were," Jarrod replied, sounding as though he had been unfairly judged over the years.

She could already tell that this time was going to cost her something... the question was what or how much. Thanks to a recent article in the local newspaper on Chuck's upcoming art exhibit in New York, Jarrod must have seen it along with Meredith's name and picture as well.

Jarrod's ability to sound so sincere, forthright and reformed was what scared her the most. Meredith and Chuck both could very easily be taken advantage of by someone with Jarrod's experience in con games, deception and theft. After all she had fallen for it once upon a time and that made her long for Doug all the more.

The last time Carla had even seen Jarrod, her father and Doug had been there too and Jarrod had *promised* that they would never see or hear from him again. Doug had threatened Jarrod that if he ever contacted Carla or *anyone* in their family other than himself, that there would be no more money... *ever*.

She wasn't even sure how often or how much money Doug had given Jarrod over the years… she hadn't wanted to know how much her naiveté had cost them as a couple and a family. Was that what this was about… *money?* Her mind scrambled trying to think of how Doug would handle the situation if he were still alive.

When she didn't respond quickly enough he said, "Just think about it Carla. I've changed a lot since the last time you seen me. I don't want anything from you… money or whatever… in fact I hate that I ever agreed to just walk away from her. I know now that no amount of money is worth sacrificing a relationship with your child." He sounded so sincere.

She felt pretty sure that Doug hadn't paid any more money to him since Meredith became an adult and graduated high school so it could still be about money… but maybe he had *finally* turned his life around. She had to be careful, for her sake and especially for Meredith's sake.

"Do you want money? Is that why you would call me now… after all these years?" she asked.

"No. No more schemes for me, I swear it, Carla. I have a job now... a good one. I realize that nothing in life worth having comes easy or free. I'm in the real estate business and even though the market is down right now, I'm doing pretty well. I think I've finally found my calling... in fact I'm looking into buying an investment property," he continued. "It's a foreclosure and I figure if I fix it up and rent it out for a few years and then sell it when the economy picks back up... I'll have a nice little nest egg for retirement. I just want to see her... just once. I'm not as young as I used to be and I just want to see her and know she turned out okay, despite... everything. She wouldn't even have to know who I really am... you could tell her I'm a friend of Doug's. Please, Carla."

"I need to think about it," she finally replied.

"I understand, but can I at least call from time to time and check in on her... and you?" he asked.

Jarrod's unique way of asking permission to continue to call and harass her for an answer was a lot to take... especially now with her heart finally working through the fact that Doug was gone. Unable or unwilling to give Jarrod permission she simply said, "I have to go..."

"I'll call you in a few days... after the holiday weekend," he finished. "Happy Thanksgiving, Carla."

As she slowly hung up the phone, she nearly jumped out of her skin when from directly behind her Greg said, "What was that all about?"

"Oh, you scared me…" she said, turning to look at him. *How long had he been standing there?* She felt a need to explain herself upon seeing the look on his face so she continued, "Oh nothing… telemarketer."

She got the distinct impression he knew she was lying to him but he didn't say anything. He continued to stare at her for several moments until she moved away to start pulling out things from the refrigerator that needed to be finished up or baked for the Thanksgiving meal she was hosting.

At least with so much to do to prepare for all the guests she wouldn't be sitting around dwelling on Jarrod Tompkins and why he had called after all these years.

"Anything I can do to help?" Greg asked still eyeing her curiously.

"Maybe you could supervise the boys in setting the table. Chuck normally does that but…" she paused upon seeing his frown, but then continued. "Chuck did at least put all the extenders in the table so it should seat twelve and he and Meredith volunteered to sit with the kids at a separate table that is leaning against the wall in the dining room. Table cloths are in the top drawer of the hutch and there are dishes and the good silverware in the bottom cabinet part."

She felt a little relieved when, after staring at her for a few more moments, Greg finally turned and headed towards the dining room. *He must be the one they sent in to interrogate the suspects because his serious expression made her want to tell the whole truth and nothing but the truth… but she couldn't… not about this.*

After setting the oven to preheat and pulling out the list of things she needed to finish preparing, she was finally able to relax and focus on the day ahead.

Meredith had asked her to host the group of bikers that she and Chuck worked with. Their boss, Bobby Jackson, lived with his grandmother, Edna, who usually hosted the group but she was getting up there in years and her house was too small to hold them all. Bobby and his wife Lilly were good people and since Lilly was pregnant it might have been a lot for them to take on anyways. Carla also adored Edna whose wisdom and patience for the rowdy group was nothing short of incredible.

Bobby's best friend Tommy McMurray and his fiancé, Dana Atkinson, would be coming with their two children, Gretchen and Melody. Greg's sister Becca Waters and her boyfriend Richard Long would also be joining them. Carla had also invited her own father and Lilly's sister, Sherri Simons, as well. So all of them along with her own family, which included Chuck and Greg at the moment, would make seventeen people but Melody was an infant and wouldn't need a place setting. So between the dining table and the small card table Carla had, there would hopefully be enough places for everyone to sit and all the women would be bringing a covered dish which would also help. It would be fun and she would enjoy the day and not worry about what Jarrod Tompkins may or may not be up to.

Once she managed to get the food ready and situated in the oven to stay warm, she went into the dining room to check Greg's progress with setting the table and was shocked to find Matt and Ben huddled on either side of him. One or perhaps all three of them had designed a football field in the middle of the table with knives, creating the entire playing field including each ten yard line.

Her glass salt and pepper shakers were being used to indicate the goal posts at either end of the field and spoons were lined up as though players for one team while forks were lined up to indicate the players on the opposing team. Greg was explaining the purpose of each player, pointing out the appropriate fork or spoon.

A stack of plates set on the hutch along with glasses and a pile of cloth napkins and rings. The table was not set because it was currently being used for the *playoffs*. She could tell her mouth was hanging open but no words were coming out. Before she could *force* some sound out Meredith and Chuck came through the front door. Chuck carried one dish in his hand while Meredith carried another one. Upon seeing the state of the dining room table, Chuck handed off his dish to Carla and walked over to where Greg and the boys were.

"That is awesome!" Chuck exclaimed, eyeing the carefully constructed playing field.

"Come on, Mom, it is best if we don't stay to watch. Gran will make them set the table when she gets here. Remember… they are a little more laid back then say the Deharts were," Meredith offered.

Edna Jackson *was* usually pretty good at getting them all to do what she wanted. Carla followed Meredith back to the kitchen still unable to close her mouth as she heard Greg and Chuck excitedly answering football questions for both Matt and Ben.

It wasn't until she had situated the food that Meredith and Chuck had brought and pulled her own stuff out of the oven that she realized... *no football!* Marching back toward the dining room, Greg was saved from the tongue lashing she had ready for him by the arrival of the other guests. It was hard to stay focused or angry when this group got together. Unlike the friends she'd had when Doug had been alive, these people were loud, shockingly inappropriate at times, politically incorrect and *fun*...

The women plus Bobby all followed her into the kitchen with their side dishes since there was no place to set stuff on the table at the moment. As soon as Bobby set the large roaster pan containing the turkey down on the counter he quickly made his way back to the dining room to watch the tabletop football game. The rest of the guys could be heard joining in on the game with opinions and suggestions.

Patting her arm, Edna said, "Just give them a minute to get it out of their systems and then they'll smell the food and then we'll see about getting your beautiful table all set for the meal. In the meantime let's see if we can get this bird carved."

The rest of the day went much smoother than the morning had with no further interruptions from the past. It was often times hard to get a word in with the group as it seemed like everyone was always talking at once, but the laughter and companionship she felt with every one of them made her feel light and relaxed by the end of the day. Even the cleanup had been fun with the women all talking together about what was going on in their lives and with their families as they cleared the table and put the food away.

Lilly's pregnancy was progressing as it should and she and Bobby were working on setting up the small spare bedroom at Edna's house as a nursery for the baby. Dana was excited over getting to be the second Lamaze coach during the birth of Lilly's baby and waiting for the arrival of a new addition to her own household in the form of a newborn foster child, even though it meant delaying her wedding to Tommy for possibly another year.

Meredith talked about the plans she and Chuck were making for a beach wedding in just a few months and how excited she was for Chuck's upcoming art exhibit at the Gallery in New York. Becca talked about preparing the spare room in her boyfriend Dickie's house to accommodate the two foster girls they would be getting before Christmas, and how nervous she was about being any type of parental figure to a child, especially at her age. Becca was only a few years older than Carla but had never had children. Being a first time parent at almost fifty years old probably *was* nerve wracking.

Much like Gran, Carla just sat and listened to them all talk, only joining in periodically but not truly sharing much. Edna appeared tired and Carla had gently coaxed the old woman to sit at the breakfast table and allow her and the other women to cleanup from the meal.

After situating Edna with something to drink and baby Melody to hold, Carla went back into the dining room to gather up the last of the dishes off the dining room table. On her way back through she glanced into the living room where the men were sitting watching football and paused mid-step.

She hadn't paid much attention to the noise coming from her living room while in the kitchen and had been instead intently focused on the conversation between the ladies. That had been her first mistake, though she would have expected more maturity from her own father. Greg was knelt down next to Ben who was standing, facing Chuck. After listening intently to what Greg had to say, she watched her little boy tuck his head down and then run straight at Chuck full speed, ramming into his waist and knocking him back several feet.

The room exploded with cheers and encouragement from the group of men. The near panic she felt that her youngest son would hurt himself was replaced with another feeling when Ben turned back around and raised his arms in victory and wearing a smile she hadn't seen since before Doug passed away. *Pride*. She felt it and obviously Ben did as well by the look he wore. So instead of breaking up the fun, even though she'd said no football and especially since they shouldn't be doing it in the house, she continued on back into the kitchen.

What felt like only minutes later, Gretchen made her way into the kitchen and said matter of fact, "That's what happens when they don't listen, I tried to tell Matt and Ben not to run in the house but they did it anyway. Now Mr. Sanders hurt his arm again because they wouldn't stop when I told them to."

Carla and Becca were the first of the group of women to make it into the living room. Her heart raced upon seeing Ben's tear streaked face from where he stood next to Matt.

Glancing around she found Chuck standing in front of Greg who was bent over clutching his injured arm. Greg's face was red with an effort to contain the pain that his expression gave away.

"Ben got carried away and tried to tackle Mr. Sanders and accidentally hit his arm," Matt supplied as she approached where the two of them stood

"I told him not to…" Gretchen said from right behind her.

"It wasn't his fault. I should have sidelined myself. I knew I was injured so I should have taken myself out of the game," Greg offered through clenched teeth. "It was a good hit, Ben, so don't worry about it."

"Matt, can you take your brother into the bathroom and wash his face, while I talk to Greg... Mr. Sanders?" Carla asked.

When the boys and Gretchen were out of sight and out of earshot Carla turned to where Greg and Chuck stood and said, "You need to have that arm examined again to be sure it didn't cause even more problems. Let me get my purse... Meredith can you stay with our guests, please?"

"We can take him over to the ER and have his arm checked out, Carla. We will keep you posted on what they say... you stay here with your boys," Dickie said. "I know Chuck and Meredith have plans later and besides, I think that boy of yours needs reassured or else he may not realize just how good of a hit that really was."

Dickie laughed when Greg smiled weakly and nodded his head in acknowledgment of Ben's great tackle. Several of the other men joined in laughing as well. Seeing that being the one to take Greg to the emergency room was an argument she was unlikely to win, she said, "Okay, but you let me know if you need anything."

Once Dickie, Becca and Greg left for the hospital, several other people prepared to leave as well including Bobby, Lilly, Edna, Sherri and Carla's father. With the house fixing to clear out she went in search of the kids and found Matt in the bathroom with his arms across his chest looking irritated.

"My mom told *me* to wash his face… not you, Gretchen!" Matt sighed in frustration.

"You should have listened when I told you to stop running in the house," Gretchen said to Ben who sat on the edge of the bathtub while the tiny girl used a wet washcloth to wipe his face off.

"You're not the boss of him, Gretchen!" Matt stated, though his previous comment had been completely ignored.

"Yea… you're nobody's boss, Gretchen!" Ben muttered his agreement.

"I *should be* the boss… because you're both too big and you act crazy about stupid football and see what happened?" Gretchen lectured them both.

Matt and Ben glanced at each other as though to silently admit that Gretchen was right. As worried as Carla was that Greg's injuries might have been made worse by Ben's horse play, watching the tiny little girl effectively curb any arguments from either one of her two boys brought a smile to her face.

She felt Dana approach from behind her and they stood in silence watching Gretchen wipe off Ben's face and then make him blow his nose into a tissue while Matt looked even more annoyed.

"Why don't I watch them and you go on over to the hospital?" Dana offered quietly.

"Oh no… I couldn't ask that," she replied.

"You didn't... I offered. You can return the favor sometime. You're obviously worried about him and I can tell you care... you should go," Dana suggested. "I'm sure having you there would greatly ease his discomfort... at least it did after his surgery."

"He has Becca and Dickie with him... he doesn't need me," she said.

A frail hand grasped her forearm and Edna said, "Take some advice from an old woman?"

She looked over at the elderly woman who had somehow appeared silently beside her and Dana and nodded.

"There is no set time limit for grief but don't spend so much time grieving that a lifetime of joy passes you by and you miss seeing it because of the tears in your eyes. When my husband died I vowed I'd never love again... and I didn't. Problem is now I wonder if that promise was worth keeping since no one ever asked it of me... especially not my Robert," Edna said. "That crippling pain will become a permanent injury if you let it."

"That's the problem," she sniffed. "I never had *time* to grieve for Doug... until now."

"Nonsense... you've been grieving every day since... and healing too. If you hadn't then your heart wouldn't have even noticed a handsome man like Greg Sanders. You wouldn't have been able to see him at all... because of the tears," Edna offered quietly. "Much like the pain that eventually dulls and is replaced with an ever present tightness when you think of someone you lost... the guilt over moving on will also ease in time."

Edna was right because up until recently the pain over losing Doug had made it impossible for her to even visit his grave. Every waking moment had been filled with a pain so sharp she often couldn't breathe... let alone cry. She had wrapped herself so tightly with the responsibility of caring for the boys and Meredith it had become a cocoon of pain and loss.

Glancing between the two women she said, "I won't be gone long. I'll just check on him and then come right back home."

"Take your time, I think Gretchen has it under control," Dana laughed.

The boys adored Gretchen and were always excited to go to outings where she would be. Within minutes of being around each other though, they were all usually arguing. Typically it was two against one but it wasn't always the boys against Gretchen.

At a considerable size difference from either of Carla's boys, Gretchen didn't let that stop her from placing herself in charge and the quicker Matt and Ben figured that out, the faster they could get down to playing.

This should bother Carla as a mother but it didn't because Gretchen was always fair and was just as willing to play along with whatever the boys wanted to do as she was to make them play what she wanted. They always had fun and usually begged to 'camp in' which was what they called a sleep over. At their ages she didn't have a problem with it and neither did Dana. To her boys, Gretchen was just one of them... and the only one who could make Chuck do her bidding.

Entering the ER Carla was met by Dickie who stood and offered her his seat next to Becca since the waiting room was full and there were no other chairs available.

"We must have been the first of many holiday accidents... this place was almost empty when we got here so they took him right back for an x-ray. If we had waited any longer to 'screw around until someone got hurt' the wait might have been a whole lot longer," Dickie said.

"He was pretty upset at even having to come here and insisted he was fine, so thank you for suggesting it. Had the idea come from me, he would probably have refused outright," Becca said when Carla sat down next to her.

"I feel just terrible about what happened and I know Ben does as well," Carla said.

"There is no need to feel bad. Greg *told* Ben to tackle him and by the time Greg realized the error of his ways, the boy had nailed him a good one," Dickie said, smiling. "Chuck's right... that kid is a natural."

They talked for a bit longer until Greg came out into the lobby area and upon seeing her sitting there, he frowned. He walked over with some papers and handed them to her. Was he angry at her for making him come here?

If he hadn't yet again interfered with her decisions where the boys were concerned, there wouldn't have been a need to visit the emergency room. She could feel her own anger over the situation mounting.

Becca looked between them and said, "Did it cause more damage?"

"No, it just hurts like hell," Greg replied.

"We were going to take the girls out for dinner this evening so we need to get going. Did you want us to take you to the beach house?" Becca asked him.

Greg glanced at Carla and she could feel the return of the tension that had been building between them since yesterday when she had washed his hair. The feeling was urgent, needy and a little overwhelming but his anger over the situation didn't give him the right to constantly butt into her business. The image of Gretchen bossing the boys around came to mind... maybe the little girl had the right of it.

"I can drop him off or take him back with me. You guys go on ahead and have a good evening with the girls," she replied in place of Greg. Somehow being bossy sounded better coming from Gretchen but Carla squared her shoulders just the same and braced for his refusal to allow her to help.

To her surprise Greg nodded his acceptance to Becca who leaned in and kissed him on the cheek. Then taking Dickie's hand, she led him outside to the parking lot.

When the big automatic double doors closed behind them, Carla turned back to where Greg stood and all the anger she felt over this whole incident rushed into her face, heating it to the boiling point. Angry or not her eyes were again drawn to his mouth which now contained a lopsided grin.

"You know if you'd listened when I told you no football for Ben, this wouldn't have happened. I expect it out of Ben... he's six! Even from Matt I could understand it, but from you? I do not need anything... any *help* from you so please," she started, but quit when he grabbed ahold of her arm with his good hand.

"I am not one of your kids whose behavior needs corrected so you can just stop mothering me. If you want to help me then I'll tell you what you can do to help... but this coddling me has to stop," he said.

"Fine... what do you need then? Are you hurting?" she asked a little breathless from her agitation and the feel of his hand touching the bare skin of her arm. *Stop staring at his mouth!*

"My arm is fine but God I ache... even worse than last night... and all I need from you is just a little... taste," he whispered before pulling her to him and capturing her mouth with his incredibly soft lips.

Before she completely lost herself in the amazing feel of his lips moving against hers... that was surely going to make it hard to sleep tonight... she pulled back away from him. She forced her eyes away from that mouth of his that felt *so good* and up to meet his gaze. Somehow she'd known those lips would feel like that... it was the reason she stared at them.

"Are you ready to go?" she said, attempting to collect her scattered thoughts.

"You don't feel that?" he asked with a look of disbelief on his handsome face.

"What?" she asked as her gaze slipped back to his mouth. *God that felt good.*

Those beautiful lips turned into a frown and he said, "Never mind… let's go."

Chapter Four

He could remember a time when he actually enjoyed being in Florida. The thought of seeing Carla usually made it a no brainer when the opportunity presented itself to come down here but that was before his failed attempts at seduction. At least the guys in the investigations unit of the Sheriff's Office back home hadn't been around to witness him being shot down. Now the state of Florida was just beginning to grate on his last nerve.

After his attempt to kiss Carla didn't go so well, he'd tucked his tail and headed off to Becca's beach house to lick his wounds. The problem was that boredom was going to kill him. At least at Carla's house there had been Chuck and the boys to keep him entertained. Here it was only the sand and beach… and solitude.

The Administrative Sergeant over his department was encouraging him to use up some of the mass amounts of sick and vacation time he'd accrued over the years but six weeks in this state felt like ten years when there was nothing to do. He might be able to take more than a year off between sick time and vacation but that didn't mean he wanted to.

The one person he wanted to spend time with while he was down here had found convenient ways to avoid him. Carla had so far sent Meredith by at the beginning of last week and then Chuck at the end of the week.

This week it had been his sister which was even worse. Becca was an attorney and a damn good one. She was constantly asking him questions… mostly about Carla… like he was hiding the truth from her… which he was, but her inquisitions needed to stop none the less. Just like with Carla… he wasn't a child that either one of them needed to take care of.

He wondered who Carla would be sending today to take him to his doctor's appointment. He could probably drive himself but between Carla and Becca telling him how unsafe driving one handed could be, he'd caved. Maybe that was part of the problem… he was always giving in to them and instead needed to take back a little control.

When his cell phone rang and he noticed Chuck's number on the screen, he sighed. He felt bad that Chuck was getting the short end of the stick by having to chauffer him around though he would enjoy the reaction of the staff at the doctor's office when they got a look at the young man.

Getting to know Chuck was a privilege he wouldn't change for anything but it was fun to watch people actually cross the street to get as far away from Chuck as they could. Fear, opinions and an unforgiving society made most people very leery of Chuck.

He had been one such person before actually getting to know Chuck and watching him step in and take care of Meredith, Carla and the two boys in an impressive way. Hell, he wished Carla adored him the way she adored Chuck.

Perhaps if he insinuated that Chuck might be the one bringing him from now on the doctor would not only do away with the sling for good but clear him for duty as well.

Sure his shoulder and arm still ached terribly and were a little on the weak side but not working was starting to mess with his head. He was one of only two people in the whole Sheriff's Office that had *actually* been shot. A couple other deputies had been shot *at* but only he and Major Laskins had actually been shot.

In fact over the past year Greg had been held hostage, testified in front of a grand jury regarding a high profile case involving Lilly Jackson's first husband, and had now been shot. All of those things had happened while in this state so perhaps he should go home and recuperate there.

"You the lucky one taking me to the doctor's office?" he asked upon answering his phone.

"No... Carla is. Isn't she there with you?" Chuck asked.

"No, I haven't seen Carla since Thanksgiving when she dropped me off at the beach house," Greg replied.

"Hold up... she hasn't been coming over and checking on you at *all*? Like last Wednesday night before church and then this past Wednesday as well?" Chuck asked clearly confused.

"No... and to tell you the truth all this solitude is starting to get to me. Do you want me to call you when she gets here?" he asked.

"What the hell is that woman up to? She must be sneaking around and doing stuff for the wedding even though we told her not to go overboard. The only problem is if she's not already there, then where is she? She should have been there by now and she's not answering her cell phone," Chuck said.

The worry in Chuck's voice had Greg sitting up a little straighter. "Everything okay?" he asked.

"Something is going on with her and I'm not sure what… but it isn't like her to lie. She left nearly two hours ago and said she had to take you to a doctor's appointment and would be back. I've got the boys but if she doesn't show up in the next ten minutes, call me back and I can load them up and come and take you to your appointment," he said. "Meredith told me she thought you and Carla were … *hooking up*… and that's what all the phone calls and sneaking around was about. So if you are hooking up I just want to know. Meredith and I don't give a shit as long as you don't hurt her. Right now I'm a little worried so if she is there… again… don't care… just don't want to freak out for no reason."

A knock at the door had him walking to the front of the house and peeking through the curtains in the living room. Upon seeing Carla's car parked in the driveway he said, "Don't worry. She just got here and I will get answers to all those sneaking around questions because it hasn't been with me."

"Good… oh and if you have a good checkup today… why don't you stop by the shop next week and take a look at what Bobby's got worked up on your bike," Chuck said and then disconnected the call.

It was one thing for Carla not to be interested in him and blow him off. It was another to use his interest in her to lie to her family and sneak around doing God knew what… *or who.* Taking a deep breath and putting his game face on, Greg opened the door and was a little surprised at his reaction to seeing her after two weeks of nothing.

Her eyes immediately dropped to his lips and before he could stop himself he said, "Window shopping?"

"What?" she asked.

"Just browsing but not looking to buy?" he replied.

"What are you talking about?" she asked, her eyes finally making their way back to his.

"The way you stare at my mouth makes me think you want… never mind," he finished quietly. "I'm ready if you are."

He followed her right back out the door to her car and the first few minutes of the trip were met with awkward silence until he decided to treat her like any other person he needed information from.

"Thanks for taking me today. Hopefully this one will be the last one or at least I can start driving myself. Then you won't have to deal with me anymore. I meant what I said… I'm still glad I asked you to help with my recovery rather than some stranger. I hope I wasn't too bad of a patient even with the unwanted advances," he said. "I also hope it didn't make your life even crazier… I know you must be busy."

"No, I enjoyed taking care of you," she replied. She was quiet for a moment and then said, "Can I tell you something and you won't tell anyone else?"

This was turning out to be easier than he expected. "Sure," he replied.

"I'm thinking of taking some nursing classes. I know it probably seems silly to do that at my age but I really did enjoy taking care of you. I think I could really help people and I need something more dependable than what my Dad can get for me up at the courthouse," she said and then whispered "I want a *real* job of my *own.*"

She never ceased to surprise him. He was expecting her to tell him she was seeing someone else… wasn't interested in him… but wanted him to cover for her with Meredith and Chuck.

"You're not too old to go back to school. You must be around my age… mid-forties?" he replied. *Stupid… Becca would kill him for asking her age.*

"I'm forty five. I had Meredith when I was only twenty and never ended up finishing college. Doug and I got married and I stayed at home with her and just when I started considering going back to school and finishing, I got pregnant with Matt. Then once Ben came along I just figured it was God's way of telling me to be content with what I had... a nice family... nice house... nice husband... nice life. Now that Ben's in school full time and with Doug gone... those old dreams just kind of came back," she said. "The problem is that I've never really worked full time and have large gaps in my employment history so even if I did get an education... who would hire a middle aged woman with no real work experience?"

"Maybe you need to take it one step at a time... check in on the classes and see if you can even get into the program first," he offered. *Great... instead of finding out where she'd been going and what she'd been doing... he was off subject.*

"Actually, I already did that. I even took the placement tests and went to orientation and I *can* get into the program... all I have to do is sign the paper and turn it in," she nearly whispered after parking the car.

"So... when do classes start?" he asked.

"After the holidays *if* I turn in the paperwork," she replied getting out of the car.

As they headed into the doctor's office he asked, "What do you mean *if* you turn in the paperwork?"

She looked at him strangely and said, "Aren't you going to ask me about when the classes are or how long they last?"

He signed himself in, took a seat next to her in the waiting room and then said, "Does it really matter? You obviously want this really bad to have held on to the dream for so long."

"It will mean having to be away from the boys even beyond them being in school because most of the classes are an hour and a half long and at night. Plus it will take me at least two years to complete the program," she answered his unasked question.

"So… you are gone for a couple of hours every night… I'm sure between Chuck and Meredith or even Dana Atkinson you can find someone to stay with them or keep them. Hell, I'd help you with them if I was going to be around. Sign the damn paper and turn it in," he replied.

She gave him another weird look and then said, "It's only two, maybe three, nights a week… not every night."

"Okay, I'm convinced… sign the paper and turn it in," he replied again. *Was she just trying to convince herself?*

"Shouldn't I talk it over with the kids first?" she asked.

"So if they proclaim that it will be too big of an inconvenience for them for you to follow your dream… you'll give it up… *again?*" he asked incredulously. *Didn't she ever do anything selfishly?*

"I'd just put it on hold again… like last time. That's all," she replied softly.

The doctor chose that moment to call him back. A half an hour later he was even angrier than he'd been on learning he'd be out on sick leave for at least six weeks.

"I'm sorry, Mr. Sanders... I can't release you in good conscious. I'm not even convinced you could draw your weapon at all at this point, let alone defend yourself or anyone else with it. You have two choices, learn to shoot left handed enough to qualify or we can bump up your physical therapy sessions and take another look in a couple of months," the doctor said hesitantly as if Greg would come after him for the words he spoke.

"Is it from my son bumping his arm a couple of weeks ago?" Carla asked hesitantly.

"No, ma'am. It's from the bullet... it looked like a clean wound when he went into the operating room but it did more nerve damage than we first thought. The surgery repaired the majority of that and it's mostly healed but some of the lasting consequences of being shot are still there and it is affecting his grip," the doctor replied. "I have to be honest... it may never be exactly the same as it was before but until he can qualify with his weapon, I cannot release him and he's nowhere near that right now."

As pissed as he was... the doctor was right. His arm just wasn't the same anymore but he could fix that... he'd bump up the therapy appointments and really start working it. He only had five more years and he could get full retirement benefits.

Otherwise he'd be forced to take a medical retirement or a desk job and since his injury hadn't been while he was on duty the chances of him getting his full benefits were slim.

He wasn't an ass kisser that would get bumped up the chain of command long enough to ensure a good retirement either... not that permanent desk duty was appealing anyways. Most of the time he pushed the limits and patience of his supervisors... but he also had the best arrest and conviction record in the whole damn division. His dream had been to retire at fifty and then ride the motorcycle that Bobby Jackson was designing and building for him across the country. He also hoped to figure out how to spend the rest of his life in the process. He wasn't ready to give up on that dream just yet but since he was screwed out of going back to work right now... he could at least help Carla work on her dream.

Now that she was at least talking to him again after his less than smooth attempts at coming on to her and since he couldn't go back to work anyways, unless he wanted to spend forty hours a week being a pencil pusher, he might as well remain in Florida. After scheduling another appointment in a month he followed Carla out to the car. She glanced at him when she got in the driver's seat as though to judge how upset he was at the doctor's report.

After Carla started the car, he placed his hand over hers when she tried to put the car in gear.

"Where's the paperwork for those classes, Carla? We aren't leaving this parking lot until you sign them. Then we are going to drive over there and drop them off and finish up whatever else you need to do to start classes after the holidays. I figure I've got at least a couple of months more down here... and I think Matt and Ben like hanging out with me. Maybe not as much as they like Chuck but I'm working on that. So I'm pretty sure you have at least three babysitters... four if you count your dad. So sign it," he finished.

The look she gave him made him want to kiss her worse than when she stared at his mouth. A mixture of excitement, joy, nervousness and wonder shone in her eyes. Then as though his thoughts were somehow transferred to her mind, her gaze went to his lips. His attraction to her only seemed to grow with each new look she gave him. The willingness to be patient and wait for her to finish grieving for her husband was completely unexpected though. Was he kidding himself? Holding out hope when there was none?

She shuffled through her purse and pulled out a folded piece of paper and a pen. After unfolding the paper and briefly scanning it she glanced at him and a smile that took his breath away crossed her face and lit up her eyes. Pressing the paper against the center of the steering wheel, she signed her name and the pressure she applied made the horn blast, which resulted in giggles from her which in turn made him smile.

When they made it to the college and parked she looked over at him and said, "I don't think I can do this after all. I'll be the oldest one in the class and it's been so long... what if I can't learn anymore. You know that saying about teaching an old dog new tricks... what if that's me?"

Without thinking he reached down with his right hand and grasped the door handle and when he couldn't open the door, it hit him. This injury could be permanent... what if the last day he'd worked as a detective *was* his last?

Looking over at Carla it struck him... she'd never even had the satisfaction of having done something she loved for twenty five years. At least he'd had that... and he wasn't giving up on going back to it just yet but he also wasn't about to let her talk herself out of her dream... again. Not after seeing that light in her eyes when she'd signed the paper.

After letting himself out of the car by using his left hand to pull the handle, he went around to her side and opened the door. Reaching inside he took the keys from the ignition and stuffed them in the pocket of his jeans. Then he reached in again and this time he grabbed her hand and tugged her out of the car.

"Wait... I need my purse," she squealed in excitement.

He enjoyed every look on her beautiful face as she turned in the paperwork and was given a list of her classes and the books she needed. Then he pressured her into going down to the bookstore and getting her books so she could look over them during the holidays. Instead of having her drop him off at the beach house, he took her up on the offer of dinner at her house. He hadn't seen her boys in a couple of weeks and since he would be down here over the Christmas holiday he needed gift ideas for them and dinner was a great time to ask.

"How am I going to tell them all?" she asked after pulling into the garage.

"You're asking me? I thought you had already aced the 'family discussion' class years ago. You're like a professional at uncomfortable conversations... but you want *my* opinion on how to tell them?" he laughed.

"Okay... the sooner the better," she said more to herself than him and got out of the car.

When they entered the house, Ben came tearing down the stairs and Greg almost felt the need to run interference between him and Carla but instead just cringed when he knocked her back a few steps by hugging her tightly around her waist.

"My teacher says I've been good and now I can play football... right mom?" he asked, holding out a gnarled paper that he had clenched in one of his meaty fists.

He watched Meredith give Carla a knowing look and before he could stop himself he was reading over Carla's shoulder. The paper was from Ben's teacher and it commended him on behaving himself better in class and turning in his homework over the past couple of weeks. However, it also said he was still struggling with his work and suggested tutoring.

Carla looked at him and even though he should take her advice and stay out of it he instead said, "He's trying... compromise and meet him halfway?"

Chuck stepped in the room with Tommy McMurray's daughter, Gretchen, right behind him. The little girl was the closest thing that Chuck had to a child of his own at this point and she was definitely his little shadow.

"Yes... you can play football but *only* if you keep up the good behavior and turning in your homework. We are also going to see about getting you a tutor," Carla replied. Again, he cringed at the brutal hug the excited boy gave Carla but the look on her face eased his worries over her ability to take his roughness.

"My Mama Dana tutors me and now I'm the best in my class. You should get tutored from her too, Ben," Gretchen advised.

Carla looked thoughtful for a moment and then said, "Guess who else has news about school?"

Meredith smiled right at Greg as though to thank him for what she was about to hear. "You?" she asked Carla.

"Yes! I signed up for some nursing classes and I start after the Christmas break. The classes are in the evenings though... after the boys get home from school" Carla gushed and then hesitated.

"Is it after football, mom?" Ben asked.

The excitement and eagerness left Carla's face in an instant when she realized that the classes would likely be during Ben's practices or games.

Chuck, in his normal fashion, stepped in and said, "Maybe it should just be you and me at football practices little buddy and your mom can come to some of the games. Moms usually just sit around worrying that you will get hurt or some shit anyways."

Ben glanced at Carla who looked away from him. It was obvious to Greg that Carla having been the center of their world and now suddenly unavailable from time to time was going to mean an adjustment for them all. As excited as Ben was to play football… the possibility of his mom not being there for it was disappointing to him. What Greg was unprepared for was the look of anguish on her face when she turned back to look at him.

"Hey why don't we go to the basement and play twister with Meredith's fake foot," Chuck offered, clearly reading Carla's mood on her face and playing interference.

"Edith's foot is not a toy… my Chuckie!" Gretchen admonished him.

It took but a moment for Meredith and Chuck to usher the three kids out of the kitchen and Greg listened as they were herded down to the basement. Carla had again turned away from him and he knew she was struggling to maintain her composure.

"I have asked you repeatedly not to interfere… and still you do. I knew I should have talked it over with them before I just made a decision like this but instead I let you talk me into it. Did you see the disappointment on his little face?" she choked.

Oh hell no… not this again. He approached where she stood and placed his hand on her arm once again and said, "So if Ben playing football would have negatively impacted Matt… you wouldn't have let him play right? Is that what you are saying? Because what I hear is that everyone here is allowed to have their own interests, dreams and goals… except you… at least not if your interests, dreams and goals interfere in any way with theirs."

"He's just a child… and I'm his only parent now. I should be there for *every* game… *every* practice because… because… Doug doesn't get to be," she replied with tears shining in her eyes.

"So you think Ben will hold the fact his father can't be there against *you* if you're not at *every* game… *every* practice?" he asked.

"No… I think Doug would… it should have been me that picked up Meredith that night. He only did it because I was watching one of those learning programs on television. He told me he knew how much I liked the show because it had to do with… *medicine*… and offered to go and get her instead. I owe it to him to do all the things he won't be able to anymore," she sobbed.

He caught her by the back of her neck and pulled her to him. *God he hated it when she cried...* he completely understood why Chuck had such an issue with it. She was so *sweet* and *kind* that seeing her cry was painful to everyone around her.

When her tears subsided a little bit he said, "Yes you do owe him that much... but that debt also includes things like fulfilling a dream, learning to live and love again, and experiencing excitement like I saw on your face earlier."

She turned away from him and grabbed a napkin out of a holder and wiped her eyes and blew her nose. When she finally pulled herself together she turned back to face him. *She was even pretty when she cried but it still bothered the hell out of him when she did.* He watched her eyes find his mouth and before he knew what to expect next, she crossed the floor to where he stood. Reaching up she pulled his head down to her and pressed her lips to his.

The fire in her kiss destroyed whatever was left of his defenses as her lips found his over and over again. Just as quickly as she had started, she broke off the kiss and leaned in one final time and rubbed her mouth against his, savoring the feel before stepping back from him.

"Thank you..." she whispered.

Now he was even more confused.

Chapter Five

It had been a week since she'd turned in her paperwork for the nursing program... and experienced a kiss that had turned her whole world upside down. *God his mouth!* Men over the age of forty shouldn't be allowed to look that good and kiss like... *he did*.

Carla forced thoughts of Greg Sanders aside because she had things to do today. She could only pray that between going back to school and what she was about to do... things would work out.

She felt like Jarrod Tompkins was making it a point to conveniently run into her whenever she went into town on an errand. Having him so close by after all this time made her uneasy because each time she did come across him in a store... or the gas station... even at the post office... it had ended up turning into a long discussion about his new life and how much he had changed.

It was terrible to think so negatively about a person, especially one who was constantly apologizing for the past, but a part of her thought it was all just a big act. That he was doing nothing more than pulling the wool over her eyes yet again.

When Jarrod called mid-week and asked if she had thought anymore about allowing him to meet Meredith she'd been ready for his interruption in her life this time. Her decision making skills might be a little rusty, especially without Doug around to talk things over with and sometimes even make the ones she didn't want to, but she'd made another big one… all in the course of one week.

Greg had forced her to make one decision on her own and it had felt good… so she'd voluntarily made another. Besides if she didn't do something about Jarrod it was quite possible that he would eventually take it upon himself to contact Meredith on his own and then what? At least this way Carla had some control over the situation.

She had taken over the phone conversation with Jarrod by imitating the way Becca spoke to people. The deal was she would take Meredith and Chuck to a store in the mall on the pretense of looking at some invitations and decorating ideas for the wedding they were trying to plan. Jarrod would approach Carla and she would pretend to recognize him as an old friend of Doug's and introduce Meredith to him.

He would then be given a few minutes to ask generic questions of Meredith before moving on. Carla had even threatened that if he in any way tried to give away more than that to Meredith, she would tell Meredith that he was crazy and that was why Doug hadn't ever brought him around.

Jarrod had sounded surprised at her ability to completely orchestrate the whole thing and even more astonished at her forceful attitude about it. *She was turning out to be a resourceful and clever girl.*

The pride she felt at making another big decision all on her own... without Doug... and the resulting smile disappeared when her thoughts drifted back to Greg Sanders. Now *he* was a clever person. He must have checked out her tale about the nursing classes and figured out that all those times she'd ended up side tracked by Jarrod hadn't been spent at the college.

He would occasionally hint that he knew more than she was saying which just made her a nervous wreck. Lying had never been her strong suit. At least Meredith and Chuck didn't call her out on them or ask her questions trying to trip her up and get her to confess what she'd actually been doing.

Telling the kids about going back to school had given her an excuse to get Chuck and Meredith to accompany her to the mall. She'd simply implied that when her classes started up, she'd have less time to help them with wedding plans.

Besides... they really did need to start finalizing their plans if they were going to be married the first week of spring. The excuse and then rationalizing her actions sounded good in theory but the deceit was killing her.

Jarrod Tompkins had been the most dishonest person she'd ever come into contact with and it felt like the more often she ran into him, the more his treachery was rubbing off on her and she didn't like it one bit. Could she even trust that by allowing him to meet Meredith this one time, he would then go away and not bother them anymore?

"You ready to do this thing, hot stuff?" Chuck asked, entering the kitchen and startling her out of her thoughts.

Ready as she was going to be to introduce her precious Meredith to the one man from Carla's past that had been instrumental in getting her arrested. Looking at Chuck and knowing the crimes of his past, which were bad... somehow didn't compare to what she had done.

Much like her, Chuck was out running his past and *that* she *could* respect... it was part of what she liked about him. She'd done the same with some help from her father and Doug. She could only pray that by helping Chuck rise above his mistakes, his past wouldn't crop back up in twenty five years to remind him that he was once young and naïve... the way her past was doing to her currently.

"Sure, let's go," she smiled.

"You ready to get your sexy on and ride on the back of my bike? Meredith is going to meet us there and I thought you could drive her car back so she and I can take a ride out to the beach where she *will* promise to obey me... for *life*," he teased.

She could only laugh at him. His constant attempts to try and get her feisty daughter to do anything she didn't want to was some form of game to him. In his mind the winning play would be to get Meredith to include the traditional love, honor and *obey* promise in their wedding vows. So far Meredith had only agreed to it if Chuck was the one who would be saying them.

Carla, having only ever ridden on the back of his motorcycle once... at a very slow speed... had also become a challenge for Chuck. Now he constantly referred to her as hot stuff, sexy mama, biker babe or some other derogatory term as a way to tease her and relentlessly tried to get her to take a 'real' ride on his motorcycle. Well, if the third time was supposedly the charm... then why not a third big decision in the same week.

"Sounds like fun," she replied nonchalantly. The ornery look on his face changed to one of complete disbelief which had her laughing hysterically.

"Are you serious?" he asked, his grin returning.

Her heart felt lighter than it had since before she lost Doug so she simply nodded. It felt good to finally get one over on the mischievous young man who would soon be her son-in-law. He picked on her constantly and it was great to finally give him back a little dose of his own medicine.

"Sweet... how about we hook you up with some ink too... maybe a piercing or two?" he laughed.

"Very funny..." she replied with a smile.

"Remind me to thank Detective Sanders next time I see him... he is the *man!* I thought Dickie corrupting Becca was awesome, but *this*... I bow to the man. Damn... and Meredith is missing it," he laughed, shaking his head in disbelief. "Here I thought you were un-corruptible but boy was I wrong! Greg has got you kissing him, riding on the back of motorcycles and sneaking around doing God knows what... what's next? Drinking? Gambling?"

"I highly doubt that... now let's go before I change my mind," she said unable to stop laughing at his antics. "I cannot believe you saw us kissing... you were supposed to be in the basement!"

"Don't worry... your secret is safe with me unless Meredith specifically asks, 'Did you happen to catch my mom planting a porn kiss on Detective Sanders?' Now, if she asks me that, I cannot lie so I would tell her the truth, but aside from that I didn't see a thing," he laughed. Then he grinned and said, "Turning kind of red in the face there, Carla."

She should have known she couldn't win at this type of game with Chuck. So instead of replying she simply picked up her purse and headed outside to where his bike was parked. He was still laughing when he came out, got on the bike and stood it up.

She put her purse strap over her head to ensure it didn't come off her arm and slung it behind her back then climbed on behind him.

Looking back at her, he smiled and then said, "You know Detective Sanders is getting a sweet ride too, right?"

"I'm not talking about Greg with you anymore," she said, looking away from him.

"Greg, huh?" he laughed and then turned back around and started up the bike.

Thanks to Chuck redirecting her thoughts back to Greg Sanders, specifically Greg's mouth and how good it had felt against hers, and the bike ride to the mall, she felt ready to get this thing with Jarrod over with. *Hopefully once and for all.* Lots of changes in her life… but most of them felt really good after suffering for so long and Greg was right… she owed it to Doug to feel this way. They met up with Meredith and Carla led them towards the department store she'd designated as the spot to meet Jarrod.

"Carla Johnson?" Jarrod said from behind them as they neared the store. *Just get it over with.*

Stopping and turning she was hit with a complete dislike for the man as she watched him look at Meredith and then move on to eyeing Chuck and finally back to looking at her.

"Jarrod, my goodness it has been a long time," she replied. *Not long enough.*

"How are you? I heard about Doug… I am so sorry for your loss. He was a good man," Jarrod said. *A better man than him.*

"Thank you. We are doing better now," she replied. "This is my daughter, Meredith, and her fiancé, Chuck."

"I'm sorry I couldn't make it to your dad's funeral… I was away on business," Jarrod said to Meredith. "You probably don't remember me much do you?" *At least he was playing his part well… but then again… being a con man had been his first profession.*

"No. I'm sorry I don't…" Meredith replied.

"Your dad and I went to school together. He was a great guy and I just know he was so proud of you. So when is the big day?" he asked her.

Watching Jarrod smooth talk Meredith reminded Carla of her own innocent response to Jarrod. At nineteen she'd been more gullible than your average teenager. She knew that… *now*. He must have seen her coming a mile away… an easy target for his schemes. Romeo Montague had nothing on Jarrod Tompkins when he found a young girl who could easily become the means to and end for one of his games. He had been too good to be true and within a couple of months he had her helping him sell counterfeit concert tickets… while having unprotected sex with her.

She'd only found out the tickets were reproductions after Jarrod left her holding the bag, so to speak. Having to tell her father, who was an attorney at the time, that she'd been arrested had been the worst experience of her life.

That incident was only matched by finding out she was pregnant. Having to tell her father about being pregnant right after he finally managed to get the charges against her dropped since she'd been unaware the tickets were fakes, was just as painful.

Jarrod probably *was* good at selling real estate... he could peddle anything to anyone... even his right to be a parent. Even now, all these years later, it still made Carla physically sick to think of the meeting between her father, Doug and Jarrod where Jarrod had agreed to leave her and Meredith alone in exchange for not being turned into the police... and enough money to leave the state of Florida far behind him. *Sorry bastard.*

Carla gave Jarrod a pointed look. Knowing his time was up, he said, "I should get going but I wonder if it might be possible to get a picture of you to show my wife? She knew your dad too,"

"Sure... I guess," Meredith agreed hesitantly.

Jarrod's one picture turned into several... one of just Meredith, a couple of Meredith and Chuck and even a couple he had Carla take of him with Meredith and Chuck. Seeing her mounting frustration at his antics he then bid them all goodbye and headed off in the opposite direction. Chuck gave Carla a questioning look after Jarrod walked away but thankfully she was saved by Meredith grabbing Chuck's arm and yanking him toward a store.

The following week was blissfully quiet with no further run-ins or phone calls from Jarrod so Carla gave a collective sigh of relief. Perhaps he *had* only wanted to meet Meredith and would keep his end of the deal this time. It would be the last she would hear from him or be reminded of her own stupidity.

Having dealt with Jarrod, she could now turn her focus to the upcoming holidays, but first she needed to stop off at the motorcycle repair shop where Chuck and Meredith worked to ask a favor.

Though she had managed to refrain from giving Greg anymore *porn* kisses, whatever that meant, it hadn't stopped her from thinking about it. Now that he was able to drive on his own, she had thought she would see less of him but that had not been the case.

He and Chuck had taken a vested interest in ensuring that Ben was the best player on his team which appeared to be just the excuse he needed to constantly be over at her house. Every time she turned around, he was there. As much as she tried to ignore her reactions to him she knew she was failing miserably.

Even her afternoon shopping trip for Christmas gifts entailed being around him. He had essentially invited himself along on the pretense that she could help him pick out gifts for her boys. He was trying to show his interest in her but the guilt over being so attracted to him was still too prevalent for her to acknowledge his flirting or return the gesture. She just needed time to adjust to the idea of being with someone other than Doug… at least outside of a couple of vivid dreams she'd experienced recently.

Pulling into the parking lot of the motorcycle repair shop, she found all the guys that worked there in the bay area. She parked alongside Lilly Jackson's car and walked into the garage. Dickie smiled at her as she approached him.

"Do you have a minute?" she asked him. "I have a favor to ask."

"You don't even have to ask… the answer is always yes. Now what can I do for you?" he said.

"Greg… he is… well he's *bored*. He is going stir crazy I think," she said.

"And driving you crazy in the process?" Dickie offered. "How about I try and get him to come down here a couple times a week and work with us. Sometimes feeling useless is the worst thing that can happen to a man. Becca told me his boss wants him to take an early retirement. Is that right?"

She didn't know how to respond to that. Greg hadn't said anything to her about that but she hadn't really asked either. With her own life so crazy this past couple of weeks she'd been so self-absorbed she hadn't even asked him about his injured arm, let alone about his job.

Truth be told, she didn't really want to know about his job… being shot at, attacked or any number of violent things that could happen to him was another reason why she wasn't really interested in getting involved with him. *Regardless of how good he was at kissing.*

"I'll give him a call later," Dickie cut into her thoughts when she didn't respond.

She thought about what Dickie had said about Greg's job the whole way over to the beach house to pick him up. He probably dealt with people like Jarrod on a regular basis. Locking up criminals had been his job for more than two decades… what would he think of her if he knew what she'd done?

Having been too enamored by Jarrod back then to really think about all the crap he had been spoon feeding her may not have made her a criminal, since there was no intent on her part, but Greg might not see it that way.

When he opened the front door for her and she stepped inside, her eyes went straight to his bare chest this time instead of his mouth. Reaching around her he closed the door but her gaze never left his stomach. He was wearing a button up shirt, which at the moment was undone, and jeans that were zipped but also unbuttoned, which left too much of him on display.

Her gaze drank him in like a sponge soaking up water. His pants hung open just enough that she could see a defined line on each side of his hips that dove down into the waistband as though pointing to his...

"When you are done looking, would you be so kind as to help button me up? My fingers aren't working so well today," he said, flexing the fingers of his injured arm.

Great... he had caught her looking at him. Why couldn't the floor just open up and swallow her whole? Her ears even burned from the humiliation.

"Sorry... I didn't mean to... stare," she replied, glancing at the floor and then the wall in an effort to keep herself from looking at him any longer.

"Look at me, Carla," he said, his voice sounding like he had swallowed gravel.

Forcing her eyes away from the wall and up to his, she faltered and found herself looking at his lips instead. A shiver went up her neck at the visual he made standing in front of her half clothed. Sexy must be his middle name and it suited him well. His mouth was an open invitation... a promise of pleasure... and his body turned that promise into a guarantee.

"No... look at *all* of me, not just my mouth," he instructed.

"I can't... I shouldn't... look... at you," she choked out. *Lord have mercy on her soul.*

"Touch me then... anywhere you want. Your hands feel like heaven, so put them on my body... anywhere. I swear to you any time I remember that night when you shaved my face and washed my hair I get hard... all over again. There is nothing wrong with it... we're both adults. Please, Carla... *touch me*," he whispered, stepping up so close to her that she could even smell the cologne he wore.

For the first time in the light of day rather than just in the dark of night when loneliness threatened to overwhelm her, she thought about touching him... tasting him... feeling his hands and *those lips* on her skin and she shivered again.

Reaching out with his good arm he grabbed her hand and pulled it over and pressed it against his flat stomach. His skin was so warm and smooth. She uncurled her fingers and slid her hand closer to his hip where that fascinating line started.

She couldn't deny she wanted him but wherever Doug was now... what if he knew what she was doing... what she was thinking about right now? The idea of hurting him... *even now*... she just couldn't. He would think she didn't love him anymore... and she did... it wasn't like that. It was just that Greg was here now and Doug wasn't... and never would be again.

"Much like the pain that eventually dulls and is replaced with an ever present tightness when you think of someone you lost... the guilt over moving on will also ease in time."

"I just can't... not yet... I'm not ready. I'm sorry, Greg," she replied quietly, allowing her hand to fall away from his beautiful body. No longer able to look at any part of him, she instead stared at the ground.

He cupped his hand around the back of her neck and forced her bowed head upwards until she had to look into his hazel eyes through the mist of tears now blurring her vision.

"I'll be here waiting when you are," he said and continued to look into her eyes for several moments before saying, "better button me up then."

Reaching out, she began to button his shirt. Why did he have to be so *kind* about it and understanding? He was absolutely *fine*... gorgeous even... and single with no kids. He could easily find someone with less baggage than her... someone younger and better looking. Settle down and have a family of blonde haired, beautiful children. Would he really wait for her? *For how long?* What would happen when he finally returned to New York to his job... went back to his life? Where would that leave her?

He made a noise and glancing up she found his head had fallen forward and his eyes were closed as though enjoying just being so close to her. Her heart constricted in her chest that this amazingly handsome man truly wanted her... *vehemently*... *Carla*... middle aged mother of three. Greg wanted her the way that Doug had once upon a time, before age and the comfort of their marriage had outweighed his need for passion.

Stretching up on her tip toes, she pressed her mouth against his briefly and then whispered, "Thank you." He felt good, tasted good, smelled good, looked good and he wanted her.

Soon. She both heard it and felt it in her soul... she would get past this pain of losing the only man she had ever loved and open herself up to the possibility of loving someone else. Or at least sharing the passion that blazed between them.

Most years she was ready for the Christmas holiday well in advance of the time, but not this year. Thanks to the craziness in her life she had one week left to finish the grocery shopping for the meal, wrap all the gifts and do the cooking, but at least the tree was finally up now.

Standing back she watched as Meredith turned the lights on. She followed Meredith's gaze to find Chuck staring awestruck at the tree. Looking at the young man's face it dawned on Carla that this may be his first holiday as part of an actual family.

Greg came into the living room with a pitcher of eggnog and lifting it up he said, "Any takers."

"Never had it before so sure," Chuck replied.

A knock at the front door pulled her away from the merriment. Seeing Becca on the front step she opened the door with a smile. The look on Becca's face erased her smile quickly as she ushered her inside.

"Is Chuck around?" Becca asked.

"He is in the living room with Greg and Meredith. Is everything okay?" she asked.

"No, but you understand… I can't..." Becca started.

Waving her hand to indicate she understood that confidentiality required Becca to only speak with her client, she led Becca into the living room. Chuck picked up on the look Becca gave him immediately and he raised his hands in surrender and said, "I didn't do it!"

"I need to talk to you in private," she said to Chuck.

"You know my life is an open book so go ahead and spill whatever it is that brings you over here. Then depending on what the problem is you can even smack me in my head if it will make you feel better. What did I do *this* time?" Chuck asked Becca.

"Violated the terms of your contract with the gallery for one… we've been served with a lawsuit! So why don't *you* tell me what you've done… canvas and motorcycles not enough *art* for you? Are you crossing over into website design now too?" Becca asked him angrily.

"Whoa! What the hell are you talking about? I haven't done any such thing!" Chuck said, the teasing leaving his voice.

Huffing angrily, Becca set her briefcase down on the couch in order to pull her laptop out of it. A few moments after opening up the laptop and typing, she set the computer down on the coffee table and turned it around for Chuck to see. On the screen was an advertisement to purchase dinner reservations to an exclusive art exhibit being hosted by Chuck.

The event wasn't one being sponsored by the art gallery and wasn't being held in New York but rather in Florida. In the center of the screen was a picture of Chuck standing next to an easel with a covered painting on it. The caption below the photograph indicated the painting would be revealed at the dinner and then raffled off. The site provided a link to purchase additional raffle tickets as only one was included with dinner reservations.

"Would you like to explain this?" Becca asked.

"I'm good at many things, but designing websites is not one of them. Besides... can you see me hosting some fancy dinner for rich fuckers?" Chuck said defensively.

Carla wanted to cry but what good would it do? Could this be the work of *Jarrod?* Maybe the only reason she hadn't heard from him after meeting up with him at the mall was because he had a new scheme. Looking closely at the computer screen, she couldn't figure out where Jarrod would have found additional photographs of Chuck aside from the ones he'd taken that day. Should she say something or was she prematurely assuming it was Jarrod?

"Just where did that picture come from then and who is planning this dinner for rich... people?" Becca asked.

"I have no idea! I swear," Chuck replied emphatically. "What I do know is that the picture isn't of me."

"What the hell are you talking about? That's definitely you!" Becca said, growing angrier by the minute.

"No, *Babe,* it isn't... I have tats and that guy doesn't," Chuck replied pointing at the screen.

Looking closer it was immediately obvious that he was right. It might be his head but it definitely wasn't his body displayed in the picture. Chuck's arms, chest, shoulders and most of his back were covered in tattoos, where the person in the picture didn't appear to have any tattoos, except for on his neck. It made no sense... whoever the person was in the picture it was either Chuck's twin or someone had done some serious editing with existing photos of Chuck.

"The right person can do amazing things with a couple of photos. So before everyone gets all in a panic, let me see what I can do. I have a buddy in the military that might be able to track down where the website is coming from and see if this is some sort of scam," Greg offered.

Becca reached over and placed her hand on Chuck's cheek and said, "I'm sorry... someday I will stop doubting you. In the meantime I hope you can forgive me for assuming. I fear you might get tired of me jumping your case all the time and just fire me."

"No one else has balls enough to climb up my ass like you do, Becca. I need that sometimes and I figure I'd rather have people around me who will keep it real than a bunch of ass kissers or gold diggers," Chuck laughed.

"Well no more assuming until I can do a little investigating and see what I can uncover," Greg advised.

Greg was right… no sense in opening up the past prematurely. It was possible there was some other explanation for the website than Jarrod Tompkins. *No more assuming.*

Chapter Six

The fact that this website involved Chuck, who meant so much to Carla, made this investigation as important as the case Greg had worked on regarding Lilly Jackson's first husband. Though it wasn't a nationally recognized case like that one had been... having it impact people he actually knew and had come to care about made it just as important. Besides, Chuck had asked him to spend the Christmas holiday with them. As much as he wished it had been Carla that invited him, he would take the chance to spend time with her no matter how the opportunity presented itself.

Knowing he needed to pull out the big dogs where this case was concerned and knowing little to nothing about websites, he called up a friend of his that was in the military. Master Sergeant Russell Hawkins had a special security clearance and might be able to get better and faster information on the website than Greg could, especially since Greg had no jurisdiction at all in the state of Florida. He had met Rusty in the police academy. While Greg had moved to New York to be near Becca and joined the Suffolk County Sheriff's Office, Rusty had ended up joining the Army instead. They had kept in touch over the years, even when Rusty had been stationed overseas.

"Hey... long time no hear, man... how's the arm?" Rusty asked.

"Sore as hell... but some days are better than others. I have a favor that I'm hoping you can help with," he replied.

"I'll do what I can but I'm actually thinking about getting out of the service… I've had enough," Rusty replied. "Seriously considering retirement… I have the years of service and I'm still young enough that I could do something else. That close call we had… just got me thinking."

"If I send you a URL could you do a little digging and figure out who is hosting the website or maybe even who created and posted it?" he asked.

"Can't your FBI boys do that?" Rusty replied.

"That's the thing see… I'm in Florida until I get medically released for duty. I am *not* a desk duty kind of guy… my secretarial skills leave a lot to be desired. So I am just taking sick and vacation leave until the doc says I can go back to doing what I *am* good at," he replied.

"I guess the scenery in Florida is better than New York?" Rusty laughed.

"You could say that…" he laughed as well.

"Send me the link and I will see what I can do… is this a security thing?" Rusty asked.

"No more like fraud or a scam scenario," he replied.

"Got it… never know what you'll run across when keeping an eye on terrorists," Rusty implied. "I'll let you know what I find."

"Thanks, man… I owe you one and happy holidays," he said before hanging up.

After getting off the phone with Rusty, Greg emailed him the link to the website and then looked around online for some holiday gift ideas for Carla. What did you get for a woman like her?

She was so kind, giving and beautiful it was hard to decide, but he needed to figure out something today because he was out of time. *Maybe he should ask Meredith for help.*

He punched in Meredith's cell phone number and waited for her to answer. Then he explained his situation and lack of options for a gift as well as his shortage of time. After hearing a muffled conversation in the background he found himself on speaker phone.

"Okay... I am with Lilly and Dana and I think they might be able to help too. It should be something really special... to show her that you are a sweet, sensitive guy," Meredith offered.

"Well I know she has a lot going on right now so sometimes the best gifts are the ones that come from the heart. How about offering to watch the boys for her while she goes to the spa or just curls up on the couch with a good book and no interruptions," Dana suggested.

"Dinner reservations accompanied by a bottle of wine would be nice. You could even find a nice a pretty necklace and drape it around the bottle... that would be romantic," Lilly proposed.

"I know she was pretty impressed by how supportive you were of her going back to school. I haven't seen her so excited in a very long time. You could give her something that would just reiterate that support... like a book bag full of school supplies... paper, pens and stuff," Meredith recommended.

They were all great ideas but which one would earn him one of Carla's smiles that he was starting to live for?

"I got her a pair of earrings that she was looking at when we went to the mall looking for wedding stuff and a bottle of her favorite perfume, so that's out," Meredith said. "The boys made a booklet of chores that they can do on their own now that she can cash in at any time, and Chuck… well it's Chuck… so he got her a gift certificate for a tattoo or piercing as a gag gift and I think he's been painting something for her as well but he's keeping that under wraps."

"I think the fact that you are asking for help is a good indicator that whatever you end up getting will have been the result of some serious thought. Keep in mind that some stores close at six tonight since it's Christmas Eve. If you get done before four this afternoon and can swing by the house, I'll help you wrap her gift before we leave for my parent's house since I've got to wrap Chuck's gifts anyways," Dana offered.

"You'll do great… just go with your gut," Lilly advised.

He thanked them all for their suggestions before hanging up and then headed out to get a gift for the last person on his list. Driving around, he sifted through the suggestions the women had given him and decided to pull at least one idea from each of them. Gift giving was never his forte but this time was even worse since, along with trying to impress Carla, he also wanted to convey his thanks for all she had done and continued to do for him. Something romantic and supportive that came from the heart… *Got it.*

Greg managed to get all three things he decided on for Carla and make it to Tommy and Dana's house well before four o'clock. Carrying his bag up the sidewalk he was met at the front door by Dana, who held it open for him.

Stepping inside he found Tommy sitting on the couch playing a guitar and writing in a notebook. Tommy nodded at him and he returned the gesture while handing the shopping bag to Dana.

Looking around he found Chuck sprawled out on the living room floor on his stomach. Gretchen, was lying on Chuck's back with her head between his shoulder blades stretched out in the same position as Chuck was in, staring up at the ceiling and talking a blue streak. Dana's youngest daughter, Melody, was crawling across Chuck's head and drooling while using his hair for balance. The whole scene looked horribly uncomfortable for the man, yet his expression was completely relaxed.

"You're just in time. I finished wrapping Chuck's gifts so I can wrap yours up real quick before I start on my own pile." Dana smiled at him and then led him into the kitchen. "This process goes much faster with Chuck providing entertainment for the girls otherwise I get a 'helper' and Tommy gets a fussy baby."

The entire kitchen table was setup like a professional gift wrapping station. Dana set the shopping bag on the table and as she pulled each gift out of the bag she smiled at him. Getting a female stamp of approval made him feel less nervous about his choices.

"These are perfect... she'll love it," Dana finally said. "Let me get you a glass of tea and you can sit in the living room with the guys... though you may prefer the couch over the floor."

A few minutes later Greg headed back into the living room, glass in hand, where he found Tommy, Chuck and the two little girls doing much the same thing as before. Chuck's eyes were closed as though he was actually napping through the torture the baby was applying to his hair. Gretchen was in the same position on Chuck's back but now wore a scowl on her face and had her arms crossed over her chest.

"I wanna go to the Johnson's house with you, my Chuckie," Gretchen complained.

"I hate it for you but it's not going to happen," Chuck replied. "Besides... you like Mr. and Mrs. Atkinson and you get to see Ben and Matt more than you get to see them."

"I'm going with *you*," Gretchen insisted. "And that's final."

"No... you're not," Chuck said as the baby used his hair and part of his cheek as an exercise ball to pull herself up with.

"Then I'm never playing with you again," Gretchen said, getting angrier by the moment.

"Fine, kiss my grits then you little shit... and get off my back," Chuck replied. "My gifts are wrapped now so I should go anyways."

"No, Chuckie! But can I go next time then?" Gretchen begged.

"I don't know... you're being awful rudy poo right now. You didn't even say 'Hi' to Mr. Sanders," Chuck said as the baby began making humming noises while trying to put her fingers in his mouth.

"Hi, Mr. Sanders," Gretchen said guiltily.

"Hi, Gretchen," he said. "I got a buddy looking into that website, Chuck. He said he would call me as soon as he had something."

"This whole thing is making me crazy because I know damn well it wasn't me that created it," Chuck replied.

"Language... *Mister*," Gretchen admonished Chuck from where she lay on his back patting her stomach in rhythm to the tune that her dad was playing on his guitar.

Watching the young man with the two little girls, it made Greg angry that someone was using Chuck's newfound notoriety for what had to be a scam. Most cases he investigated involved strangers that he only knew as a name on a report. The people down here were more like... *friends*.

They helped him out without ever expecting him to pay them back. Greg crossed his fingers that Rusty would find something for him to work with. Chuck may look like a hardened criminal but he was a good guy and didn't deserve for someone to take advantage of him, if that was what the website was about.

Once Dana finished wrapping the gifts for him, he thanked her and then drove back to the beach house to collect his other gifts to take over to the Johnson house. Greg realized halfway to Carla's that he no longer felt weird or like the odd man out around the group of bikers.

He had wondered why someone like Carla and even his own sister would be friends with such a rowdy group of people but he completely understood it now.

Since being wounded, these people had visited him in the hospital, brought him food, gave him advice, wrapped gifts for him and recently even invited him to come down to the motorcycle shop where the guys all worked to get him away from all the estrogen... or so Dickie had said.

After the holidays Greg might just take the man up on his offer... get to know him on a personal level... especially since it was looking like his sister might end up marrying him. He knew Dickie was a good man, had sensed it right away, and had even been rooting for him to win Becca's affections. So it was time to really get to know him.

Perhaps having somewhere to go, even if it was only for a couple of days a week, would take his mind off the conversation he'd had with his boss. The longer the physical therapy continued on his arm, the more Greg was starting to realize that it was quite possible that it would never be one hundred percent again. Major Laskins must know that but also knew there was no way Greg would go for an administrative job like the one he held. The retirement proposition was a good one but to take it felt like admitting that such a big part of his life was over. The badge had been his wife for twenty five years... that's a long time to be with the same woman. What would Greg do when *she* was gone too?

The Major had made it sound like an offer but he knew the political bullshit well enough to know if his arm, and more specifically his grip, didn't improve soon he would be facing a choice. Being tied down to an office and a desk or taking the retirement package he'd been offered.

Quite honestly the whole situation just pissed him off... but there was no for better or worse in his marriage to law enforcement. Worse was being shot and injured... but thankfully not killed... but it was still grounds for divorce.

Becca was moving down here to Florida permanently and telecommuting with her office. When she was needed for court she would fly back to New York. In fact she was already living with Dickie and they were even taking in two little neighbor girls who were in the foster care system. That meant that even if Greg did get cleared for duty again, he would be returning home alone. He had friends on the force but most of them were already married with a family so their commonality only went so far.

Pulling into the driveway at Carla's, he gathered up the gifts he planned to go ahead and put under their tree this evening and headed up the walkway. After knocking a couple of times, he realized that she wasn't home. He hadn't thought to call... actually he was just getting used to hanging around... *invited or not.* It was bad and he should in all reality stop it... in the words of Chuck, he was being a stalker. This place just felt... homey... not just a house with four walls and roof and that was thanks to Carla.

He put the gifts in the trunk and got back in the driver's seat. He wasn't sure where to go but he didn't want to go back to the beach house and sit there alone on Christmas Eve... not this year. He also wasn't about to call Chuck and ask where Carla was since it wasn't really his business. His sister and Dickie were spending time with their two foster kids so that option was out too. Dana and Tommy had already left to go out of town by now.

That left Bobby and Lilly but by the time he made it across town to their neighborhood, he'd changed his mind. He didn't want to crash their family time either, especially during the holidays.

Sometimes being single sucked. This was a family holiday and aside from Becca, who was also busy, he didn't have one. He was out a family and potentially a job as well. Twenty five years and all he had to show for it was the ability to drive around in a not so good section of town with gifts in the trunk of his car without fear.

Finding a bar a few blocks from where Bobby and Lilly lived with Bobby's grandmother, Edna, he pulled in and went inside for a drink. The woman working behind the bar was Lilly Jackson's sister, Sherri Simons. Sitting down on one of the barstools he watched as Sherri approached him.

"What brings you in here?" she asked.

"It's a holiday and I'm single," he replied.

"Well, first one is on me as thanks for what you and Becca did for my sister. I've never seen her so happy... so what'll it be?" she asked.

After ordering his first drink he sat there mulling over his job. Then his thoughts went to Carla Johnson as each song on the jukebox made him think of her. Then his mind pondered his current bachelor status, Carla Johnson, his aching shoulder, and of course, Carla Johnson again.

Sherri was a damn good bartender and kept the drinks coming until he knew he was looking at either sleeping it off in his car or calling a cab which would not do since he needed his car to take the gifts he bought to the Johnson's house the following day... *to Carla's house*.

He looked around for Sherri to close out his tab after realizing how long he'd been sitting there drinking and finally found her off in the corner behind the bar talking on the phone.

While he waited for her to finish her conversation, he watched a couple dancing and envied the man. *That* man wouldn't be alone this evening... *Christmas Eve*... even if it was just for one night the guy wouldn't be alone.

Greg on the other hand would definitely be alone because the woman at the end of the bar who had been watching him most of the night wasn't his type. *That* woman didn't have a man's haircut that showcased a slender neck which begged for his kisses. She didn't stare at his mouth and it was doubtful her touch could make him beg for more... not like Carla at all. He was *way* drunk. *Great.*

A few minutes later Sherri approached him again and gave him his tab. He pulled his wallet out with his left hand since the alcohol didn't help the crippling effects of his gunshot wound. Handing her his credit card, he watched her set it near the register and proceed to serve every other customer at the bar before finally cashing him out. He signed the receipt she gave him and turned around in his seat to try and crawl to his car. He was met by Carla Johnson's disapproving eyes. *Shit!*

Reaching around him, he watched as Sherri handed Carla his car keys. She must have pilfered them along with his credit card. *As if he would really try to drive like this.* Then she also handed Carla his wallet. Dropping both items in her purse like a disapproving mother, Carla again gave him a look that said more than her words ever could.

"I would have expected more out of you, Detective," she said sarcastically. "Can you walk?"

"Yes… I don't need you to mother me, Carla," he huffed. His words even sounded slurred to his own ears.

Looking back to Sherri, who now smiled the smile of the devil, he wanted to tell her how unfairly she had treated him. She had led him down this path by supplying him with one long unending drink and now she laughed at his misfortune. And in front of Carla Johnson no less… why would she do that to him?

Before he could say anything, Sherri said, "Yes, I am a bitch but someday you will thank me for this… just not tonight."

He turned back to Carla when he felt her attempting to pull him off the barstool using one arm around his waist. One of the wise men he was not, because this was likely the stupidest thing he'd ever done in his life. Getting drunk in New York where he would have taken a cab to the bar and would therefore have to take one back home was a whole lot different than leaving a rental car with a trunk load of gifts in the parking lot of bar on the seedy side of town... in Florida.

"I will just sleep in the car tonight... because your Christmas is in my trunk," he said. *Gifts... gifts in the trunk.*

"Why didn't you bring them by the house before you came here to drink yourself silly?" Carla asked as she guided him out the door of the bar.

"I did come home... and you weren't there," he said indignantly. "I mean your home." *Mental note... he was not a good drunk.*

"We went over to Doug's parents for their Christmas celebration but we were home by nine," she replied as she guided him into the passenger seat of her car. *It smelled like her in here.*

She got in the driver's seat after transferring the gifts from his car to hers. Once she'd pulled out of the parking lot she glanced over at him and said, "So is all this drinking because of your job?"

"That's part of it... but it's also about *you*," he replied. *When had Whiskey become a truth serum?*

"*Me?* What did I do? Drinking yourself stupid is a *personal* choice... not something another person can *force* upon you," she said defensively.

"You don't do anything. That's the problem," he muttered under his breath.

"I have been really busy getting ready for school, entertaining the boys while they are off for winter break and getting ready for the holidays. Besides... you said that you didn't *need* my help anymore," she explained.

"I *don't* need your help..." he replied sarcastically.

"You are a hateful drunk... do you know that? If you don't want my help then what? What do you want from me?" she asked angrily.

"I want you beneath me... I want to feel your body enjoying mine. I want you to kiss me... not just stare at my mouth. I want you to stop mothering me and treating me like another one of your kids! I'm a grown man, dammit! I want you to tell me that I even stand a *chance* with you!" he replied.

He'd done it now... she stared straight ahead for the rest of trip. When they pulled into her driveway, he realized too late that she intended for him to stay at her house. Again, she looked over at him and he felt her disapproval like a blanket covering his head. *Smothering him.*

"I know you're not a child and I know you're not... Doug... but sometimes old habits are hard to break," she said quietly. "Truthfully, I just want to help *you*... but *I'm* the one who needs the help. Who am I kidding?"

"What could you possibly need help with? You run this household like a professional event planner. You're sweet, funny, sexy and smart. You're *perfect* so what could you possibly need help with? You're not facing a forced medical retirement after twenty five years or Christmas Eve alone," he replied with the sound of self-pity ringing in his ears.

"You're right about that," she sighed. "But I *am* facing a past that has come back not only to haunt me but make me sorry all over again."

"What are you talking about?" he asked. *He sounded like he was slobbering... good grief.*

"Perfect?" she laughed. "I'm a far cry from it and unfortunately my daughter and Chuck may end up paying the price for my flaws."

His head may feel like it was wrapped in cotton but his heart told him this was important and despite the white noise the alcohol was creating he sat up straighter and listened.

"I have never admitted this to anyone else except my father and my husband but I was arrested once," she said and then looked away from him.

"For what?" he asked.

"Selling counterfeit concert tickets," she replied.

What? No way! Even his alcohol saturated brain couldn't accept what he was hearing. The admission coming from her was like the strongest coffee and acted as a way to sober him up. Turning towards her in the seat he was just in time to see a single tear spill down her cheek.

"Recently?" he asked.

"No! No, when I was nineteen," she confessed, looking down at her hands. "I was conned into it by the same man I think is responsible for that event website regarding Chuck."

"And who would that be?" he asked. His heart was numb at her confession.

"Jarrod Tompkins... but I need you to promise me something," she nearly whispered. "If it is him and you catch him, I need you to let him go."

What? Her confession became more confusing and crazy sounding by the minute. He was a cop! Why the hell would he let a suspect go if he was able to catch him, especially one that had done something to her own daughter and future son-in-law?

"Why the hell should I do that, Carla?" he asked.

"Because the man is Meredith's biological father... not my Doug," she choked. "And she must never know that. Promise me."

"You are asking me to break the law, Carla! I can't do that... *even for you*," he replied.

"I'm not asking you to break the law... I'm asking you to shut down that website and then walk away... don't get involved beyond that," she said. "I'm asking you for Chuck *and* Meredith's sake, please, just let it go. I will figure out a way to pay those people back who bought dinner or raffle tickets... I swear."

"I can't... *because* it's Chuck and Meredith," he said. "And because it's you."

Chapter Seven

Would he even remember her confession from last night? Seeing Greg drunk had made her feel really bad for leaving him alone on Christmas Eve while she and the kids were at Doug's parents' house and also sympathetic over him being potentially out of a job.

Then, as if she were drunk herself, she'd confessed all to him. She had started talking and it was like opening a window to her soul... sharing with another person... *besides Doug*... and she couldn't seem to close it back shut. It had felt so good to unload some of her burden on another person. Now she could only hope that Greg had been drunk enough to either not remember it or think it had been a dream or just his imagination.

Finishing up the cinnamon rolls she was making for breakfast and putting them in the oven, she headed to her room to get a shower and dressed for the day before the boys got up... or Chuck. The young man had been so excited about Christmas morning that Meredith had to basically drag him upstairs to the spare bedroom by joking that Santa wouldn't come if he wasn't in bed fast asleep.

Carla had been somewhat thankful that they'd still been awake when she got home with Greg, or she might never have got him in the house.

Laying her clothes out on her bed, she then opened the door to her attached bathroom and was startled out of her thoughts at the sound of the shower curtain being pulled to one side.

Looking up she was gifted with a sight she'd only ever imagined. Standing in her shower was over six feet of finely chiseled Greg Sanders, with drops of water sliding down his muscular shoulders and carved chest. Before her mind could advise her differently her gaze lowered and, rather than a quick glance, she looked her fill.

"Let me know when you're done looking and I'll dry off and get out of your way," he offered.

"I'm sorry…" she whispered, her throat suddenly dry. *She was still looking because she just couldn't seem to stop.*

"No need to apologize… ready to touch me yet or are you still just window shopping?" he asked.

She'd been so lost in thoughts of the coming day she must have missed the fact that he was no longer asleep on her couch in the living room and instead she now stood staring at him… *all of him. And wow was he a sight.* Forcing her mouth closed and her eyes back to his, she watched him remove a towel from the rack and run it roughly over his hair with his left hand, watching her as he did so.

Incapable of speaking, she stared as he stepped out of the shower and walked over to where she stood. Unable to handle the heat shining in his eyes she instead looked at his perfect mouth. He stopped in front of her and bent until he was able to again capture her gaze with his own. Handing her the towel he then guided her hand and the towel to his chest.

"How about a compromise then? You can look all you want but I get to feel you… even if it is through a towel," he whispered.

Every nerve in her body was awake now and reaching out toward him. Forcing her hands to move, she wiped the towel down his beautiful chest while he dipped his head lower. He ran his delicious mouth along the column of her neck and across the skin of her shoulder that was exposed around the strap of her nightgown.

The sensation streaked down her body and settled between her legs causing her head to fall back on her shoulders and a guttural noise to escape her lips.

"You mentioned last night that you were the one who needed help. I think you need a lot more than just *help*, Carla. I think you need a man's touch… *my touch*. You watch my lips because you know they can help make your body come alive again… like your touch does mine," he whispered against her shoulder before scraping his teeth along the bone and sucking on her skin.

Through the fog from his hot shower and the haze in her brain she heard Ben's voice upstairs. Greg must of heard it too because he lifted his head. Moving his mouth to hers, he placed a kiss on her lips while staring her in the eye.

"Shower is all yours. I'll finish up breakfast while you get ready," he said against her mouth. Then he pulled the towel back out of her hand and left the bathroom, closing the door behind him.

How long she stood there unable to move from enjoying the tingly sensation that was now pooled between her legs, she was unable and certainly unwilling to admit. She listened as he got dressed in her bedroom and then eventually left that room as well.

She managed to shower and was nearly dressed before catching sight of a painting Chuck had made of Doug for her. This time instead of the normal sadness she saw shining in Doug's eyes, which the painting captured so well, she could see a smile there instead... as though he accepted what was happening between her and Greg. Instead of jealousy or disappointment that she would have expected to see, the painting instead reflected... *relief.*

"Merry Christmas, Doug. This year I will do better at making sure that the kids... that *I*... enjoy the holidays. I promise," she whispered.

She could swear she saw approval in Doug's eyes that stared at her from the canvas. Smiling at the painting, she headed across the room to her bedroom door before realizing that the feelings Greg brought out in her weren't *replacing* the love she had for Doug... they were *enhancing* it. Allowing her to remember what it felt like to live again... to love again... *for them both.* Glancing back over her shoulder she smiled again at the painting. *An unspoken goodbye.*

She barely made it down the hall from her room when Chuck and the two boys came barreling around the corner and stopped short in front of her.

"Maybe we should open gifts first, before breakfast... I mean as good as it smells we should let them cool down some first," Chuck suggested.

Matt shook his head in agreement of Chuck's suggestion and Ben looked as though his whole body was full of excited approval.

"Sorry, mom... I tried to stop him but he's worse than the boys," Meredith called from the kitchen.

Looking at the three of them she couldn't stop the excitement that settled in her stomach... the joy on their faces was contagious. Sighing heavily she said, "How about one gift each before breakfast?"

As quickly as they had appeared they disappeared back into the living room and she could hear them sifting through gifts under the tree. Meredith's laughter rang through the house as it had before Doug's death. A feeling of contentment settled around her shoulders like a cloak of comfort as she followed behind them a little slower. Greg had been right... this is what Doug would have wanted for them all. *Especially for her.*

Watching them inspecting their gifts and trying to decide on which one to open before breakfast, she felt Greg approach her and leaning in he said, "You still seem pretty perfect to me."

He *had* heard her confession... *all of it*... and much like with Doug, it hadn't mattered... hadn't changed his opinion of her one bit. Doug had loved her unconditionally... regardless of her past... was it possible that a police officer could as well? Just as she was about to ask if he wanted the gift she'd got for him, he pulled his left arm from behind his back and held out a gift bag on the end of his fingers.

"Open mine first?" he asked as though reading her thoughts.

The kids all stopped, even Chuck, and stared at her. Taking the large gift bag over to the loveseat she sat down and pulled out a beautifully wrapped present from within it.

After carefully un-wrapping the box she opened it to find a teddy bear dressed as a nurse. Around the bear's neck was a lovely gold chain with a pendant of the Red Cross indicating the nursing profession. The stuffed animal also held a clipboard which had a note attached asking her out for dinner sometime before her classes started and a gift certificate to an office supply store.

Between his looks and *this*... how he managed to still be single at his age was a complete mystery to Carla. The boys quickly lost interest in the heartfelt gift she sat holding and went back to looking under the tree at their own gifts. Seeing they were distracted Carla met Greg's warm smile and sensual gaze.

Leaning over she kissed him full on the mouth. The passion between them that always lay just beneath the surface was still there, but this time she felt more than the incredible sensation of physical attraction. An unexpected connection to him she had thought she would never again share with another person... *another man*... sprang to life.

The rest of the morning simply flew by and she felt so lighthearted watching the boys and Meredith enjoying the holidays again after such a dark and painful period in their lives. Chuck's reaction to the holiday was refreshing and brought home the charitable idea behind this time of year.

It felt like the sunshine had finally broken through the clouds and was warming her... much like Greg's mouth against her skin.

The following week the New Year was celebrated while trying to both prepare for the trip to New York for the premiere of Chuck's art at the gallery and have everything in place so that she could start school as soon as they returned from the trip.

Greg didn't say anything more to her about her confession where Jarrod was concerned but she knew he was still working on the case. She had even overheard him talking on the phone a couple of times. The only difference now was that whenever he was working on it he would cut phone calls short if she was around as though keeping it all a secret from her, which she didn't appreciate.

Doug had done similar things during their marriage as though she wasn't capable of making those kinds of decisions and so shouldn't be bothered with the particulars of the situation. Instead of being frustrated over the issue, she instead focused on packing up the boys' things so they could stay with their grandfather since school would be starting back up for them while she was in New York with Meredith and Chuck.

She had somehow become the event coordinator for the whole group and did the best she could to book hotel rooms and dinner reservations with the account information from the gallery that Becca gave her. The gallery was hosting and paying for up to ten family members or friends of Chuck as part of the premiere. He and Meredith were too excited to think about hotel accommodations for the group or how to get around the big city or even food.

Apparently she could make sound decisions for ten people about where to stay in a huge city in a whole other state but couldn't be trusted with information about skeletons from her own closet.

Having made it to her father's house to drop off the boys in record time thanks to a lead foot filled with annoyance over Greg shutting her out on his investigation into the website, Carla helped the boys carry their things in the house. She had finally broke down and told her father what was going on and had been surprised at his change of heart from the first time they'd had to discuss Jarrod Tompkins.

Back then he'd been angry and had tried and been successful at sweeping the whole thing under the rug. Twenty five years later he sounded guilty for giving Jarrod money and a free ride out of town and trouble.

"I've often wondered when that judgment call would come back to haunt me. I can't say I'm any more ready for it now than I would be in another ten or twenty years, but I'm ready to end this thing for good this time," he'd said.

The funny thing was back then she'd been ready to take her lashes for her part in the whole fiasco and her father had been the one insisting they make it go away quickly and quietly. Now it sounded like he was in agreement with Greg about finally dealing with it while she was the one wanting to sweep it back under the rug.

Maybe this time *she* would be the one to stand on the rug in hopes of keeping it all neatly tucked beneath. Entering the kitchen she watched her father abruptly end his phone call and brace himself for Ben's over eager hug.

The boys dragged their bags down the hallway and into the bedroom they shared when spending time with their grandfather. A few minutes later she could hear the sounds of one of their favorite video games starting up.

She made herself a glass of tea and refilled her father's glass then sat down at the small table that set between his kitchen and the living room. He took a drink and stared at her over the rim of his glass.

"Just got off the phone with Detective Sanders... seems they were able to shut down the website and have in fact tied it back to one Jarrod Tompkins," he said. "Somehow I doubt that son of a bitch will go away quietly this time even if we paid him off again, Carla. Chuck's an opportunity Jarrod can't pass up... his biggest score yet. Have you considered just telling Meredith the truth?"

"It would devastate her... with the accident and everything. I should have listened to my gut and told her about Jarrod back then when Doug and I first discussed whether or not we should. Doug was her *daddy*... I know that and that's not why I even brought it up," she sighed. "This right here... right now... is why I thought we should have told her the truth. Their bond was thicker than blood... she was his *world* and I don't think that would have changed if she had known about Jarrod. With the accident, I'm afraid it would crush her. She says she no longer blames herself but it would seem like rubbing salt in an open wound to tell her now."

"That girl is like your mother was… delicate and fragile to the naked eye but tougher than nails when it really counts. You cut her short by believing otherwise. Think about it like this… it may not even be an option much longer. Besides staring at you like a lovesick fool… hunting down criminals and locking them up is the *second* thing Greg Sanders does better than anyone else I know. Better for Meredith to be gently introduced to the idea than to be smacked in the face with it," her father said.

She was exhausted. After kissing the boys goodbye she drove home to try and get some sleep before the caravan to New York left in the morning. Instead, she lay there thinking about the conversation between herself and her father. In most things she trusted her father's judgment but always she felt it was Doug's decision to tell Meredith because he had loved her so much. With him gone that decision now rested squarely on her shoulders and it felt like a betrayal to Doug to tell her now that he was gone. It was an even bigger betrayal than looking at, kissing or thinking about Greg Sanders *naked*.

The following morning she picked up Dickie and Becca on her way to the beach house to get Greg. The happy couple was only a few years older than her but watching them together made Carla a little jealous. She'd had that kind of relationship with a man once, the only difference being that Doug had been the head of their household while in this case it seemed like Becca was in charge. The petite woman often seemed to pick up and take over where Bobby's grandmother, Edna, left off and Dickie was content to allow it. Dickie pampered Becca almost as much as he teased and flirted with her. They were cute and sexy and immediately made Carla think of Greg Sanders and her growing feelings for him.

"Why don't I take the first shift driving," Dickie offered when they pulled up in front of the house.

Becca headed up the walk and returned a few minutes later with Greg following behind her. Once they were all situated in the car with the men up front and her and Becca riding in the backseat, they hit the highway.

The rest of the group would be meeting up with them at a hotel halfway between Florida and New York that Carla had reserved rooms at. The others were all riding together in a van that Tommy had surprised Dana with for Christmas. The trip was long and only made longer by the tension that continued to build between her and Greg. *Always building and never releasing.*

A simple look from him felt just like his mouth on the skin of her shoulder and it was slowly making her crazy. At the same time he seemed to have put some distance between them. Perhaps his sanctimonious need to always error on the side of the law had him rethinking his attraction to her after all. She might not have ever been convicted of a crime but she had in fact committed one... *unknowingly*... but she had. Well that was fine because, honestly, she had enough on her plate with this trip and school starting in a couple of weeks to have to worry about him anyway.

The following morning after reaching New York they went down to the first floor to one of the hotel conference rooms for a private breakfast buffet that Cameron St. James had setup as a planning meeting. Entering the room, her eyes were immediately drawn to Lilly Jackson who looked way too good to be almost nine months pregnant. She was laughing hysterically as Chuck knelt in front of her and guided her hands to pull her shirt tight against her belly. Then Chuck sat back on his heels and, completely ignoring the frightening scowl Bobby was giving him, encouraged Bobby to stand behind Lilly and place his hands over hers. Then Chuck began to draw in his ever trusty sketchbook. Meredith stood behind him with her hand on his shoulder, watching and giggling as badly as Lilly.

Tommy had his arm around Dana's waist leaning her backwards while he appeared to be feeding her grapes from the long buffet table between stealing kisses. They were smiling and laughing at each other... *playing*.

Off to the side Becca sat with Cameron and his assistant Daniel at a large round table talking quietly. Dickie stood behind Becca periodically running his fingers along her neck which she tried unsuccessfully to swat away. This only brought about a smile from the handsome older man.

Just as Carla was about to find a seat somewhere and just watch the group, who apparently acted the same no matter if they were riding motorcycles around their small Florida town or about to attend the social event of the season in downtown New York City, she felt Greg approach her.

"I find myself strangely at ease around all of them… like I've known them for years," he said, stopping right next to her. "The only tension I feel in this whole room is right in this area here," he continued, motioning the space between their two bodies. "Sadly, I am about to make that feeling worse."

By the time his words registered he had begun walking toward Cameron St. James. She found herself following him and only stopped when he approached the table and said, "When you have a minute Mr. St. James, I have some information on that website that I think you will want to hear before tonight."

Damn him! *Why now?* He wasn't even being paid for this investigation and even though she had nearly begged him, he'd not let up until he had figured out all about the website *and* Jarrod. Had he caught Jarrod? Was he about to spill her deepest secrets to Meredith in front of the whole group? Looking around she watched as the merriment died down and the others made their way over to the large table and sat down.

"By all means, Detective, shall we step out in the hallway?" Cameron asked, looking first at Chuck and then Becca and then finally to Greg.

"No sense in all that, there's no one here that won't find out the whole story by tonight anyways so have a seat and spill it," Chuck offered. "They're family."

"The website was a scam orchestrated by a man named Jarrod Tompkins," Greg said, sitting down at the table.

Forcing herself to follow suit, Carla sat down at the table. Although the bigger part of her wanted to run, especially after both Meredith and Chuck recognized the name and looked at her.

This must be what the saying meant about sticking someone's feet to the fire because Carla felt physically sick to her stomach. Only anger ranked a close second. Why couldn't he have waited to say something in private?

"He managed to get a photo of Chuck and then paid another man to manipulate that photo with another photo of himself standing next to the easel," Greg explained to the group who were now quietly listening with rapt attention. "Then he created fancy looking invitations that also contained an edited picture of Chuck, which he then gave to individuals and couples who contacted him through the website and purchased what they thought were dinner reservations and raffle tickets for one of Chuck's paintings."

"I would assume that you were able to catch up to the man..." Cameron said angrily.

"Actually no... not yet," Greg replied. "We will though... it is only a matter of time. In fact... we think he may have come to New York hoping to sell more dinner reservations and raffle tickets to those who didn't get an invite to the premiere."

"So how big of a scam are we talking about here?" Daniel asked.

"Dinner reservations were two thousand apiece or three thousand for a couple. Each reservation came with one raffle ticket per person and extra raffle tickets could be purchased for a thousand dollars apiece," Greg replied.

Carla just wanted to cry but instead sat in shock over the potential amount of money involved as well as the thought that someone could do that to their own blood whether they actually knew the person personally or not. Smearing a person's good name for her own personal gain was a thought that was just simply beyond her. *How did the bastard live with himself or sleep at night?*

Having cheated maybe twenty people out of a hundred dollars twenty five years ago ensured she never missed a Sunday service and even all these years later she often prayed *again* for forgiveness. Jarrod Tompkins saw each person he came into contact with as a potential new mark.

Even Chuck had once told her he wished he could tell the store clerk he had robbed at gun point how sorry he was for what he'd done. Never once had Jarrod been sorry for what he'd done... even now to his own daughter and her fiancé.

"We were able to track down about twenty couples so far who each purchased between two and six extra raffle tickets as well. So this man has effectively conned people out of more than one hundred thousand dollars," Greg continued. "However, I wanted to let you know before the authorities begin contacting all these people and telling them there isn't any special dinner and no painting, because even though Chuck had nothing to do with it and knew nothing about it... he does have a record. I fear those affected by this may think he was in on the scam *based* on that record... and how he... *looks*."

The room grew suddenly quiet with each person lost in their own thoughts that someone had taken such horrible advantage of their friend. Most of society would think these bikers were the ones to watch out for, not a clean cut man in a business suit.

People's willingness to judge would possibly make Chuck a victim all over again in this and some would say he deserved it for what he'd done in his past but not her. Carla knew him for the fun loving young man he was now.

He had breathed life back into her household and into the very daughter whose biological father was responsible for all this. How could she possibly tell either him or her daughter that ultimately this was her fault? She couldn't... she just couldn't. She felt the tears spill over just as Dana handed her a Kleenex.

"Who in the *fuck* would pay that kind of money just to have dinner with *me?*" Chuck asked. "I mean seriously... even with the chance at winning a painting... for that kind of cash they should be getting a little *something, something*, to go along with it."

Several snickers were heard around the table. Though Carla should no longer be as caught off guard by the things that came out of Chuck's mouth by now, she was and choked out a laugh. A couple other people also laughed behind their hands.

"Actually that's about what the guests at the premiere paid for tickets to this event," Cameron interjected, obviously attempting to contain a laugh.

"Isn't there something we can do? Those people got bent over minus some lube! Way more than I *ever* ripped someone off for... Maybe you can pimp me out to *their* families like Nathan did to me with my probation hours," Chuck suggested to Greg. "Hell, it might take me a little while but I could probably paint them all a small painting or something."

"Oh no!" Cameron exclaimed. "You cannot save the world, Mr. Reynolds."

"I feel bad, dude!" Chuck said, throwing his hands up in the air. "Sometimes, it's not always about money!"

"Wait! Everyone just take a deep breath here…" Becca ordered, looking at the people gathered around the table. "What's stopping *us* from going ahead and hosting this dinner and raffling off a painting? If we know who the victims are and how many tickets each person should have… Chuck can still donate a painting to be raffled off. We can all scrape together enough food and help to host a meal for all those people can't we? Hell, Carla did it by *herself!*"

"Becca's right! We could even publicize it and state that any additional proceeds will benefit a charity and maybe even open it up to more people. Then it cuts the cost involved and makes Chuck out to be the hero in all this instead of… the alternative," Lilly exclaimed. "*Someone* refuses to let me work at the shop until the baby comes and I need something to do with my time, so I can help. I used to do this kind of thing all the time."

"You can count us in too. Chuck and I can sit down and figure out a charity that he feels deserves whatever extra funds do come out of this and contact them," Dana suggested, smiling at Chuck. "Maybe that will help inspire him to paint something specific for the event."

"I can keep track of how much extra money we bring in and the cost involved hosting the dinner," Meredith offered.

Carla felt overwhelmed by the women of this group who were offering their time and assistance for something that had nothing to do with them. They wouldn't receive any benefit at all for their efforts but they did it to help a friend.

Even though they didn't realize this was her fault, somehow she knew it wouldn't matter. For the first time since losing Doug she felt like she had someone... several people actually... to rely on.

"I'd be happy to prepare most of the food. I have a friend who owns a catering business who might be willing to help us out at cost since it would be for charity," Carla finally managed to say after absorbing the feelings of warmth and caring coming from the group.

"I'll talk to Sherri about bar tending for the event and maybe Tommy and Gretchen can provide the entertainment," Lilly said. "Dickie and Bobby can work on finding a place to hold the event and setting up for it. Chuck and Tommy can help with that part too."

"Cameron and I will see about providing some legitimate publicity for this and perhaps something special for the victims," Daniel offered.

"One thing ... we do this my way this time. I'm doing this whole suit and tie bullshit for you guys. *This* event is mine!" Chuck said with a smile.

Chapter Eight

Somewhere between announcing to the group about the scam, eating breakfast and listening to Dickie and the guys talking about how to raise more money for the charity to cover the money that Jarrod stole, Greg lost sight of Carla. He only looked away for a minute and by the time the guys got done discussing ideas for fattening the pot, as Dickie put it, the women were gone. *Damn it!*

Greg still hadn't actually told Carla the worst part, though she may have already figured it out. Chances were good that Jarrod would either be at the premiere or at the very least nearby.

"Did you see where Carla went?" Greg asked Chuck.

"They took off in a hotel van to some fancy *spa*. Meredith almost talked my dumbass into going along until Lilly said something about getting waxed. I'm some dumb but not plumb dumb. What's a Brazilian Wax anyways… and ain't that shit for chicks?" Chuck replied, looking a little confused.

Greg didn't really take in all that Chuck had said until he made it over to where Dickie stood to see if Becca might have told him what spa they were all going to. Stopping and then turning back to look at the young man, he couldn't help but cringe a little bit at what Chuck would be subjected to later this evening.

Then again, perhaps he should be more worried about what the guests at the premiere would be subjected to when they met Chuck. Some weird part of him was looking forward to the shock and awe the upper class guests were about to receive from this whole group... *especially* Chuck. They would get a show along with a chance to view some of the most incredible art Greg had ever seen.

"No idea but they are getting the *works*, whatever that means," Dickie replied, waving his hands as though clueless when Greg asked him about the women. "I can only guess that means it will cost a small fortune and take up most of the day."

That just meant that now was as good a time as any for Greg to go take care of signing the paperwork for his retirement. He'd negotiated the best deal he could get out of this whole shoulder injury, both professionally and personally.

Though he had wanted to put in the full thirty years, he knew lots of guys opted to get out at twenty five years and some ended up on medical retirements long before that even. It didn't make this any easier.

Excusing himself from the group, Greg headed to the parking garage of the hotel to get Carla's car and drove to the Sheriff's Office one last time. Parking and heading inside he was surprised that instead of the nostalgia and disappointment he thought he would feel, he was actually excited about retirement... at least a little bit.

Sometimes change was a good thing... right?

Stepping inside the bullpen area, several guys he'd worked with for years smiled at him and Sergeant Miller headed over to him and held out his hand. Shaking the offered hand, Greg watched the sergeant's face drop a little and he looked pointedly at Greg's shoulder. Was it really that obvious... sure his grip wasn't as good now and he had a small shake in his hand sometimes but...

"Good to see you, Greg. You came in just to sign over that bike those boys down south are building for you, didn't you?" Sergeant Miller teased with a laugh.

Laughing in return, Greg replied, "Not a chance, but I *did* come to sign those papers that will allow you to replace me."

"Some things just can't be replaced. You're one of those things. I mean these past couple of years you have really made a *name* for yourself and this department. That means something to the whole office and to all of us who still work here so if you ever need anything... just give a call," Sergeant Miller said, grasping Greg's shoulder and guiding him towards his office.

Realistically, being shot or at least shot *at* was all just part of the job, but the case against Lilly's first husband had been a nationally televised one. That investigation and trial had been high profile and a life changing event in more ways than one. More than likely it had jump started the danger Becca had recently faced. So taking a bullet for his sister rather than in the line of duty was somehow more fitting.

Without that one single case there would be no custom motorcycle and no Carla Johnson.

Greg followed the sergeant into his office and closed the door behind them. He sat down in the chair across from the man and watched as he visually inspected the differences in Greg, post gunshot wound. After shuffling through a stack of papers and finding the one he was looking for, he glanced at Greg once more before handing the packet of papers to him.

"He's definitely in town for your buddy's premiere... the guys tracked him to a hotel near the gallery. I guess it goes without saying that we can't do anything until we catch him making a sale here. Since this has now become a federal case... my hands are tied until something actually happens in my own backyard," Sergeant Miller said.

"You're going to make sure the guys out there and even the Feds are ready to bring him in at the first sign though, right? That was the deal... that sorry bastard in return for me signing this," Greg said, first indicating the guys all standing around out in the bullpen with his thumb and then waving the retirement paperwork around with his other hand.

"Already on it... consider this as going out with a bang, Greg. I did have one last favor to ask," Sergeant Miller said, leaning back in his chair and eyeing him thoughtfully. "Any chance you'd take Trina to that gallery thing tonight? This might just make up for the lousy birthday gift I got her last month."

Trina was Sergeant Miller's little sister whom Greg had dated at one time. She'd dumped him once she realized that there wasn't really any glitz or glamour to dating a law enforcement professional… just a lot of time alone.

When a Wall Street broker had caught Trina's eye with his flashy sports car that was all it had taken for her to hit the road. Trina was sweet but not really Greg's type anyway. Sergeant Miller was an old friend and regarding that Greg had a lot in common with the bunch of bikers that Carla and Becca associated with. He would do next to anything for a friend and Sergeant Miller was no exception.

"Yea, have her meet me out in front of the gallery at seven thirty and I'll get her in the door but beyond that…" he replied.

"Oh, I know… besides she's still with that goof from up town. I just know that she's recently taken an interest in expensive art and with your *connections* I thought you could help my popularity points with her. That's all," Sergeant Miller said.

They talked a while longer about recent cases and of course the incident involving Lilly, the motorcycle the guys in Florida were building for Greg and what he'd be doing in his spare time now that he was retired. Then Greg took the pen the sergeant offered, sealed the deal with his signature, and headed back to the hotel to get ready for the premiere at the gallery. Twenty five years… done… just like that. This must be what divorce felt like.

Greg had turned in his service weapon to the sergeant just before leaving the Sheriff's Office for the last time but he'd run by his apartment on the way back to hotel and picked up a gun of his own. He may now officially be a *retired* police officer but the sergeant had known Greg wouldn't be able to stand around and watch someone like Jarrod Tompkins scamming more people out of money. So he formally requested Greg's assistance with this one last case.

So just in case, Greg would have a weapon with him to protect and serve at least for this one last time… especially since it involved Carla Johnson. Sergeant Miller understood that about Greg and knew he *would* get involved if Jarrod showed up tonight. So rather than leaving Greg out of it… on his own as a civilian… Sergeant Miller had instead asked Greg to assist in any way possible. It was a thank you for taking Trina to the premiere tonight and was much appreciated.

Greg showered and managed to get dressed, all except for his tie. Every day something new cropped up to remind him that he wasn't the same man anymore. Tying a necktie was just another one of those tasks that he wasn't as good at now. Maybe taking his sidearm tonight wasn't such a good idea after all… if he couldn't dress himself, shooting accurately and timely was an illusion. Sighing in frustration he headed down the hallway to Carla's room and knocked on the door.

The woman who answered literally stole his breath and left him unable to form a rational sentence let alone ask for help. She held the door open for him and he somehow managed to make his feet walk into the room. It was just a classic black dress but on Carla... it was absolutely *exquisite*. Two wide straps covered her breasts and wound up and around her neck which along with her short haircut and dangly earrings only accentuated her beautiful skin.

The dress tapered down to fit her slim waist perfectly and then flared out to end at her knees where the fabric swirled around her legs as if inviting his gaze to linger there.

"Need some help?" she asked, pulling his tie loose from where he'd draped it around his neck.

Stepping up close to him she reached up and pulled the collar of his dress shirt up and he was assaulted by the perfume she wore. It was warm and spicy and whispered to him all the things he should do to her... *for her*. He could feel her adjusting the tie around his neck but couldn't concentrate on anything but her beautiful eyes that focused on her task, the catch in her breath at being near him, and the delicious sight of her exposed skin in that dress.

Pushing his jacket off his shoulders she said, "Here, let's take this off first. It might make this easier to tie and then you can put it back on."

He allowed her to undress him, then she shook out his jacket, stepped back from him and turned to walk over to one of the beds to drape the suit coat across it. That's when he saw it. Her back... all that luscious skin was bare from her slim neck all the way down her back to her waist.

The legs that had just moments earlier been useless to him made it across the room to where she stood next to the bed in mere seconds. One of his hands reached out and covered her bare upper arm to hold her steady.

"Carla... that dress looks amazing," he managed to choke out before his need to taste her overruled his common sense.

Leaning down he rubbed his lips across one bare shoulder blade. She arched forward as though she'd been scalded and cried out in a noise his body recognized as pleasure. Had his hand not been holding her by one of her arms, she might have fallen but instead he was able to keep her from getting too far away from him.

Her skin was a delicate treat he couldn't remember experiencing before with any other woman. He rubbed the tips of his fingers against the exposed area he'd just tasted. Again she tried to arch away from him and another noise escaped her beautiful mouth.

Deciding he wanted more than anything to hear more of those sounds coming from her, he stroked the backs of his fingers from the base of her spine all the way up to her neck and was rewarded with a full body shiver.

"Please stop that, Greg... I can't take it... and remain standing for much longer," she begged. "Your mouth feels as good as it looks."

"Then let me taste you some more... *all of you*," he whispered against her neck.

"No... I can't. Not right now," she whimpered.

God not this again... he was a patient man but he was also burning alive. She might still be grieving but she was also hotter than any of the women in their twenties he'd dated before meeting her. Sensual must be her middle name with the way her whole body had reacted to his touch.

"Then when..." he whispered, licking a patch of skin on the back of her neck that made her entire body shake.

Before she could answer him or he could apologize for pressuring her there was a knock on the door. He felt like curling up in a ball and just crying... his body didn't just *want* her... he *needed* her. Carla pulled away from him and stumbled over to the door as though she was drunk and opened it to Chuck and Meredith standing in the hallway. *Damn it!* He liked the young couple... most of the time... just not right now.

Looking around Carla to where Greg stood, Chuck said, "You guys ready to do this thing?"

"Let me help Greg with his tie and we'll be all set," Carla replied quickly.

Then she walked over to him and in a few short moves had his tie done, his collar back down and was handing him his suit jacket. It felt like a dismissal but Carla was right. They needed to leave to ensure they made it to the gallery on time. Cameron and Daniel wanted Chuck there a few minutes early.

Meredith looked beautiful in a silver colored floor length formal dress that hid her prosthetic, though Greg doubted any man would be able to look past the dazzling smile she wore… especially when she looked at Chuck. He was a little surprised that Chuck was dressed in a suit. It was better than his normal attire but he wasn't fooling anyone and he wasn't anywhere near as formal as the guests coming to see him would be.

As much as Greg wanted to be alone with Carla it would have to wait because he couldn't begrudge the happy couple this night even if Carla *was* willing to allow him to explore her incredible physical reactions to his touch.

He helped Carla cover up with a warm wrap since the weather in New York was much colder than in Florida this time of year. They made it down to the lobby where they met up with the rest of the group and for the first time he felt like the odd man out.

The men were all dressed in nice jeans and shirts while the women wore formal gowns like Meredith and Carla.

Lilly Jackson looked stunning for being so far along in her pregnancy but the difference between her and Bobby was even more evident based on how they were dressed. She wore a long, flowing red dress that somehow made her belly not seem as big and round.

Either way she was a beautiful woman and Greg had to appreciate the way Bobby kept staring at her. Bobby on the other hand wore a button up shirt and jeans that were both black and there was no tie.

Dana Atkinson approached Chuck and gave him an excited hug. Greg had never been attracted to redheads but the teal colored dress that Dana wore made her eyes really stand out and her mass of hair had been carelessly swept up off her neck and piled on top of her head.

Of all the women, Dana would blend in the most with the guests at this party. She was polished looking and between that and her height she had a couple of men in the lobby checking her out. Tommy stood next to her looking like Bobby's twin with a nearly matching outfit.

His sister, Becca, stood next to Dickie off to the side wearing a floor length navy colored dress. Something about Dickie's posture made Greg take another look until he realized that the man must be doing or saying something inappropriate because he was grinning while Becca was blushing and avoiding eye contact with anyone. Dickie was perfect for Becca… he pulled her out of her sometimes frigid shell.

Stepping up next to Carla, Greg placed his hand on her back as the group collectively headed outside to the waiting limousine. Instead of moving forward with him, she took a step away from him and positioned herself next to Meredith.

He would have been offended if her next move hadn't been to look over her shoulder at him… her eyes almost immediately dropping to his mouth. He was still torn between loving that look and hating when she did that. It was reassurance that she wanted him but it also made him even crazier for her.

When they pulled up in front of the gallery and got out, his eyes scanned the crowd gathered outside waiting for Chuck. Years of experience drew his gaze to Jarrod Tompkins like a flame in a darkened room. He was standing in a heavy group of people off to the side of the entrance. For most people he would have gone undetected but Greg still knew what he was looking for... retired or not. Glancing at Carla he noted that she was too involved with Meredith and Chuck and therefore Jarrod's presence went unnoticed.

As Greg started towards Jarrod hoping to get close enough to see or hear what the scumbag was discussing with the couple he stood talking to, Greg was startled when someone put their arm around his. Looking down he was surprised to find Trina Miller smiling up at him. Apparently to a twenty eight year old excited woman, seven thirty really meant seven o'clock. *Great!*

A sound from Carla brought his head back around. Meeting her gaze he was surprised to read hurt in her eyes. Her eyes then focused on Trina who was giggling in her excitement. *Shit!* This was not what it looked like. Actually it kind of was what it looked like... Trina was here with him but as a *favor*... not a *date*. Before he could say something to explain himself and quite possibly make the situation even worse, Carla moved forward with Meredith and Chuck.

In his moment of distraction Greg lost sight of Jarrod and when he looked back the man was gone. Greg followed the group inside after Becca passed by him giving him a dirty look from where she clung to Dickie's arm. The rest of the members in the group wouldn't look him in the eye once they made it inside. Fortunately the awkward moment was quickly replaced with excitement when Cameron and Daniel approached Meredith and Chuck and quietly gave them some instructions.

A few short minutes later the doors were held open and the guests began to filter into the main gallery where a large portrait of Meredith hung on a faux wall. Lights hung down and shone onto the painting making the shadows and colors stand out even more. The wait staff, dressed more elegantly than Chuck and his friends, meandered around offering the guests champagne and hors d' oeuvres.

Sometime later Greg looked around for Carla and much like the first time he'd ever seen her, she was wandering around the gallery looking at Chuck's paintings in wonder. As soon as Trina spotted a young couple that she knew she let go of Greg's arm and wandered off to mingle with them. He took the opportunity to approach Carla.

"I went by the office earlier while you were out with the girls and Sergeant Miller asked if I'd mind bringing his sister, Trina, to the premiere this evening," he said by way of explanation to her unspoken question.

Instead of looking relieved as he'd hoped for or forgiving as he expected, Carla's facial expression didn't change at all and as if she hadn't heard a word he said, she turned and simply walked away.

Something akin to panic settled in his stomach. Normally he would attribute her actions to being jealous but the fact that she didn't hurry away, act mad or any of those typical reactions he would have anticipated drove his anxiety over the situation up to a whole new level. He found himself following her across the room while attempting not to actually chase her down.

Just as he neared her, Dickie stopped him by placing his hand on Greg's arm. "I heard what you said to her... just give her a minute to swallow the realization that she wants you enough to care that you're here with another woman. Step back from it and let her come to you."

"She thinks..." he nearly whispered. "When the reality is I want her so bad I can hardly think of anything else. Trina really is just a favor to a friend... I swear."

"I understand that, believe me... and yea... she does think *that* and it is bothering the hell out of her. Not jealousy really... just the idea that she needs to decide if she is ready to feel like that again and if she wants you in return or if she should let you move on to someone else. Give her time to make that decision on her own and it'll be worth it," Dickie replied, smacking Greg encouragingly on his upper arm.

Then the older man turned and walked away from Greg leaving him staring after the thing he hungered for to the depths of his very soul. *God this was killing him.* It was hard to be patient when everything about her made him want her... especially her earlier sensuality. *Good God*! Being with her was all he could *think* about... touching her... tasting her... *loving her*.

Deciding he should stop torturing himself and keep an eye out for Jarred Tompkins instead of panting after Carla, he was headed toward the front of the gallery when a disturbance caught his eye. After all these years... even after the case against Lilly's first husband... he hadn't learned anything.

He again had let something... *or someone*... distract him and now Jarrod Tompkins stood talking to Chuck and Meredith. Meredith looked shocked and Chuck looked angry and like normal... Carla was one step ahead of him. Make that several yards as she hurried towards where Chuck stood looking as though he was about to...

"No, Chuck!" Meredith said loudly, clutching Chuck's arm and attempting to pull him back and away from Jarrod Tompkins.

"I'm telling you both the truth!" Jarrod insisted. "Just ask her... they made me leave. I swear to God!"

"I'm so gonna kick your ass if you don't shut the fuck up and leave right now," Chuck ground out between his teeth.

Carla stopped only a couple of feet from Jarrod and stared at Meredith who merely glanced at her and then went back to attempting to keep Chuck from laying the man out by standing between them. Greg had always wondered how Chuck ended up with a criminal record for a violent crime since he was normally so easy going. The fierceness of the young man now made the idea a little more believable.

As Meredith continued to try and push Chuck back, the rest of the guys in the group were suddenly surrounding Jarrod and just as he thought all hell was about to break loose, a couple of deputies he'd worked with came through the door.

Greg watched them place Jarrod in handcuffs as a couple entered the gallery and pointed out Jarrod to another officer and proclaimed him to be the man who they had just given money to. This was not how this was supposed to play out. *What happened to quietly?*

"I swear it to you, Meredith... it's me... not Doug Johnson... *me!*" Jarrod said loudly as he was led out of the gallery followed by the latest couple to be taken advantage of.

Daniel followed the officers outside and after the gallery cleared out some, the guests, who already considered themselves above the law, continued on as though nothing had happened. A couple of women in expensive designer gowns eyed Chuck and the other guys from the group as though they were a decadent desert. Apparently being on the wrong side of the law was just as big of an attraction to women as wearing a badge... even to upper class ladies.

Chuck continued to eye the door that Jarrod had exited through as though struggling not to follow the police officers outside and pound Jarrod into the ground... regardless of the presence of law enforcement.

Meredith held on to both of Chuck's arms. Sensing she wasn't having the impact she needed to calm him down, she suddenly captured his face in between her hands and kissed him. Quickly the kiss drew attention from onlookers as the young man went after Meredith instead of Jarrod... just in a different way.

After a moment, Dickie cleared his throat and then laughed at the expression on one man's face who appeared to be completely shocked at the open display of affection between the young couple.

"Give it a try for yourself... she'll appreciate it," Dickie suggested to the man, pointing at the man's date.

The man took his date's arm and turned away from the group but the woman looked back at Dickie curiously before being dragged away. Dickie was laughing at Chuck's antics right along with Tommy and Bobby. Greg started across the gallery toward the group after thanking the lead detective on the case and assuring that the man had his cell phone number to keep him informed. Carla intercepted him about halfway to where they all stood.

Tears shimmered in her eyes along with anger and disappointment as she placed her fragile hand on his chest to stop him mid-step.

"I have asked you... *repeatedly*... not to interfere with my family... with my kids. Now you have interfered in something that is *none* of your business. I should never have told you *anything* about my life... about my past. Now my own child knows how badly her mother screwed up and will be forever impacted by that man. Do you understand that? How dare you, Detective? *How dare you?*" she hissed at him.

Before he could fully appreciate all the passion in her tirade at him, she raised her tiny hand and slapped him a good one. The strike didn't hurt but it effectively knocked out the remaining control he held where she was concerned. Grabbing her by her upper arms, he did just what Dickie had suggested he *not* do.

He kissed Carla... not the hesitant hopeful kisses from before but a declaration of his feelings for her... an insistent kiss that spoke of his hunger and intentions toward her. His mouth forced hers to submit to him and open for his invasion.

The only thing that brought him back to his senses was the feeling of being watched. That and Carla clutching his head between her small hands holding him to her while his mouth made its way down the delicious skin of her neck toward her shoulder and the sound of her whispering, "How dare you, Detective... how dare you do this to me?"

Chapter Nine

Releasing her arms he pulled back from her and she felt the loss just as she'd felt it when Doug had left... *died*. This time was by choice... unlike Doug... Greg Sanders had *chosen* to do this to her.

Greg's gaze captured hers and he sighed before saying, "I only just signed my retirement paperwork this afternoon. Up until that point my job *required* me to report any and *all* crimes happening in this state. In Florida, I'm a guest... a visitor... with no obligation to get involved but here... I *am* obligated. I didn't interfere to hurt you, Meredith or Chuck! I did it because I'm a cop and because I care about you... all of you... you and your kids."

"You're mouth looks so good and kisses incredibly well but it is by far the best at *lying*," she said hatefully, forcing her gaze up to meet his hazel eyes.

Instead of arguing with her, Greg removed her hands from his shoulders and backed away from her. She could see signs of anger and hurt, much like she was feeling, reflected in his eyes. He had only himself to thank... she had nearly *begged* him to look the other way about this... but *no*.

Now he wanted to be upset because it had worked out the way she somehow knew it would when she'd asked him to back off this case... not look into it too deeply. He turned away from her and walked over to the gorgeous young woman he'd come with tonight, who stood looking at the group like quite a few of the other guests. *He could take the woman home... it didn't really matter now... did it?*

He said a few words to the woman and then they just walked out of the gallery. A sensation deep in her heart told her that it might very well be the last image of him she would ever see. It couldn't be helped... she had to look out for the kids first. There would be time enough for her to live again when they were grown and out of the house. Then she could find someone... hungry kisses that set her body on fire were *not* a necessity.

Carla watched Chuck say something to Dickie who placed an arm around Meredith's shoulders and led her across the gallery and down a hallway leading to Cameron's office. Becca remained behind and quickly took Meredith's place right next to Chuck who finally looked to be back in control of himself. A few guests who had stood around with their mouths open staring at the group and all the commotion continued to stare at Chuck.

"What?" Chuck finally asked a couple of them defensively.

That seemed to be the motivation the guests needed to move away and continue touring the gallery. *What could she say to Chuck?* As though he didn't have enough issues of his own, her past had shown up tonight to ruin the evening for not only him but the whole group! *How did a person apologize for that kind of drama?*

She was nearly directly in front of him before he actually noticed her there. The tears were right there begging to be released but she didn't deserve to give her emotions free reign... she needed to do what she could to make this up to Chuck... *somehow*.

Chuck had become like another one of her kids over the course of a few short months and she hated disappointing him as much as she hated disappointing Meredith or the boys. Unable to voice her feelings, she instead held her arms out to him.

He stepped forward and hugged her tightly, nearly lifting her off her feet and said, "I'd have fucked him up real bad for you back then, Hot Stuff... so he best be glad he only had to deal with Nathan and Doug."

"I'm so sorry for all this, Chuck... this was supposed to be *your* day and I've ruined it," she choked out.

"No, babe... you didn't ruin anything, but let me give you a tip. Sometimes when there are just too many skeletons to store in your own closet, kicking them back in and trying to hold the door shut doesn't work. You have to take a few out and pass them off to one of your buddies to hold for a few days," he said, finally releasing her. "Some hot ass chick I'm fixing to marry is hanging on to a bunch of mine so I got room to store a few of yours if you need it."

Carla patted Chuck's cheek as the first tear made its way down her face. Turning away from him, she was approached by Dana who put a thin arm around her shoulders and led her across the gallery to the office that Meredith had disappeared into. Carla could hear the clicking of Lilly's heels on the tiled floor right behind them as if she was coming along for moral support.

It was time to face her demons... clean out her closet a little bit. However, Carla would never forgive Greg Sanders for forcing her to do so *tonight* of all nights.

Just as she stepped through the doorway of Cameron's office and Dana released her, Chuck's words hit her like the slap she had delivered to Greg earlier. Thoughts of Greg's lips moving against hers threatened to take over and she had to force them away. *Never doing that again.*

What she needed to focus on was the fact that somehow Chuck knew about her father and Doug having dealt with Jarrod before. *How in the hell did he know about that?*

The realization then hit that if Chuck knew then it was quite possible that Meredith did as well. Carla brought her gaze up to look at her beautiful daughter's face. It was there in Meredith's eyes that glistened with unshed tears... in the strength showing in her slender shoulders which she'd squared in preparation for this conversation... in the way that Dickie had his hand on Meredith's upper back to show his support. Who had told them? *Greg Sanders! That bastard!*

"What did he say to you?" Carla asked in an effort to buy herself some time.

"Nothing I didn't already know. He just confirmed it and that explains why you and Daddy never told me about him," Meredith said as a couple of tears spilled down her cheeks.

"What do you mean you already knew?" Carla asked in shock.

"Come on, Mom! You and Daddy weren't even *dating,* let alone married, when I was born and there are no pictures of him holding me as a baby... only you, Grandma and Grandpa. I figured it out in about ninth grade but I just thought you guys would tell me eventually," Meredith explained. "Then when college hit and I saw how proud Daddy was of me for going to the same school he did... I just stopped caring about who, what or why... especially after the accident. *Doug Johnson* was my daddy... *is* my daddy... he always will be."

"I wasn't as smart in *my* youth as you are. I let a smooth talking man... *boy*... talk his way into my heart, then into my bed and effectively change the course of my whole life," Carla managed to blurt out. "The only thing he ever did for me was to get me arrested and teach me a valuable lesson about judging people on appearances. And he gave me you... so I couldn't *hate* him. Even now... all these years later but he's no good, Meredith. I should have told you... admitted how badly I screwed up back then and maybe none of this would have happened with Chuck and the website. I'm so sorry, honey."

"Chuck said that day at the mall that there was a story there between you and Jarrod but I didn't know what he meant and even when Greg figured out it was Jarrod that made the website... I didn't put two and two together. It's time to stop covering for his sorry ass, Mom. He isn't anybody to *me* so I hope they stuff him in a small cell at the back of the jail," Meredith smiled. "You've always been the pillar of our family and I love you for it but I'm a grown up now... I can take it."

"I'm sorry... I should have told you years ago but when I wanted to say something your daddy didn't want to and then when... he died... I just couldn't. Is there anything you want to know about Jarrod?" she asked.

"Not about him so much... I don't know him and based on the website and what I just saw out there... I don't really want to know him... but I am curious about one thing?" Meredith replied. "How are you even still *alive* if you got arrested? I mean I would have thought Grandpa would have grounded you for the rest of your life."

At hearing Meredith's laughter and the look on her face, a relief flowed through Carla as though she'd been holding her breath for the past twenty five years. It was strange how the once cute little girl who had been so instrumental in bringing her and Doug together had suddenly grown into a woman who resembled him the most out of any of their kids. Meredith's heart was good and her will strong. With Doug's help they had raised a woman the world couldn't help but stand up and take notice of.

"Yea, I'd have thought ole' Judge Patterson would have given you at least a thousand hours of community service… maybe even *two* thousand," Chuck said as he walked into the office.

Turning back to look at the young man whose art spoke of a wounded soul capable of healing other souls like his own, Carla could only smile at his antics. Always one to lighten the mood since emotions were so hard for him if not expressed on a canvas. Chuck was such a key part of their family it was as if Doug had hand picked him to look after Meredith after the accident.

In life Doug probably wouldn't have approved of Chuck but he had only ever wanted Meredith's happiness and Chuck provided that for her. She felt Doug's approval… as though he still had an influence on all their lives… but rather than the usual pain she felt when thinking of him, the idea just left a strange but beautiful sadness in the spot where only unbearable grief used to reside.

"I really thought Daddy would string me up that night when he came to bail me out of jail. He simply said I could either learn from it or I would be destined to repeat it. Needless to say I learned from it… at least for the most part. So I guess you finally understand why he never just blew *you* off as a lost cause, huh, Chuck? He recognized in you a *want*… a *need* to change your life's path. Just like that scared twenty year old girl I was all those years ago," Carla replied.

"Grandpa really paid Jarrod to leave?" Meredith asked incredulously.

"Yea... it was *wrong* but... yes he did," Carla replied honestly.

"Good... because anyone who would take money in exchange for their child is the one who is *wrong*," Meredith said and then hugged her. Carla knew she'd been forgiven.

She watched Lilly and Dana share a look between them and then look back at her. Carla was grateful for their support, both of herself and Meredith.

"So are all you ladies ready to head back out there? I guess I get *two* hot chicks for the evening since Sanders hit the road with *Barbie*," Chuck said, eyeing Carla thoughtfully.

Carla had been *dreadfully* hard on Greg for absolutely *nothing*... for doing what he thought was right. Why was it she could be so forgiving to almost *anyone*... except for him? A feeling of guilt over what she'd said to him settled in her stomach but what could be done about it now? He'd left with *Barbie,* all grace and curves made for a fashion show runway, after having received a scolding from Carla... middle aged mother of three.

"I know my brother pretty well and as tough as he may seem most of the time... chances are good he's at his apartment licking his wounds," Becca supplied from the office doorway.

Did she have the guts to go to Greg and apologize for being so overprotective of her kids that she'd unfairly lashed out at him? Would he forgive her for being downright *vicious* toward him? All she could do was try to make things right with him again.

Greg had become a true friend to her... sure she'd helped nurse him back to health... but he'd been her staunchest supporter for going back to school and finally getting a degree. In the back of her mind Carla pictured showing up at his apartment door only to have the young blonde who had to be closer to Meredith's age answer his door instead of him. How could a middle aged mother of three even hope to compete with *that?*

"Go get him, Tiger!" Chuck laughed. "Give him another one of those porn star kisses and he'll kick Barbie to the curb."

"Enough, Chuck, please. I came here to support *you*, not to..." she said, and then realizing they were all staring at her, instead just headed back out to the gallery.

Halfway across the tiled floor of the main showroom she again noticed the beautiful painting of Meredith. Each color and shadow spoke of the painter's love of the model. A return of affection was there in the flush showing in the small sliver of Meredith's cheek that could be seen and the shy bow of her head.

Carla felt that way when Greg Sanders looked at her and his kisses told her he felt the same way in return. The painting was about reaching out for love... admitting it and waiting on a response.

She stopped dead in her tracks and glanced back at Chuck with a real understanding of just how incredible his paintings really were… they spoke to the soul. *The beautiful canvas whispered words of encouragement and hope.* The smile and wink Chuck gave her assured her that no matter the value of his paintings or how famous he became… he would always just be Chuck Reynolds… biker and *friend*.

Just like Greg Sanders would always be a cop… retirement wouldn't change that. She needed to let Greg know that she understood that concept now. Asking him not to get involved had been like asking him not to be who he was.

Becca touched her arm and handed her a business card with Greg's cell phone number and address on the back.

"Do you have money for a cab?" Becca asked her.

"No… I, uh," she hadn't thought to really worry about money since she assumed they would be at the gallery all evening.

"Please… allow me," Cameron insisted and guided Carla out the door as Daniel guided Meredith and Chuck over to meet an expensive looking couple.

The ride to Greg's apartment building had every nerve in her body on alert. She wasn't young like *Barbie* so she wouldn't pretend not to know where this night would end if he in fact had gone home *alone*. He'd begged her to touch him and this time she was ready… why should she deny herself any longer.

Doug was gone now and had *never* asked her to remain alone and celibate should he die first. Not to mention, two of her four kids approved of Greg. Realistically *all* the kids liked him. Aside from that... *she wanted him*... with every fiber of her being she wanted his touch.

The cab driver offered to wait for her so getting out of the vehicle she approached the callbox on the wall near the front entrance and hit the button for his apartment number and waited. After a minute or two had passed, she pressed the button again and after several more minutes she tried one last time. When she still received no response she got back into the cab.

She couldn't go back to the gallery... she could but she wouldn't... *didn't want to*. He *was* with *Barbie* and her heart both hurt and was angry all at the same time because she hadn't grabbed the opportunity when she had his full attention.

She gave the driver the name of the hotel and sat back in stunned silence fighting off disappointed tears as they made their way slowly through New York traffic. Greg had finally lost patience waiting for her. It hurt... *like hell*. Aside from his stunning good looks, he had stood up for her chance at school and unlike Doug who always encouraged her to play it safe... Greg had encouraged her to step out of her comfort zone... *dared* her to go for it. It had been unexpected but had felt... *wonderful*.

That excitement in her stomach had felt like jumping off the high dive for the first time and Greg had caught her before she splashed down... had an answer for every excuse she could come up with.

After exiting the elevator Carla started down the hallway towards her room at the hotel until, unable to stand the sickness in the pit of her stomach over having lost her chance with him, she decided to detour down another hallway just to see if he was by any chance in his room. At the very least she owed him an apology... then she would go and leave him and *Barbie* alone. She was setting herself up for serious disappointment, she knew that, but couldn't stop her feet as they carried her to his door.

She knocked on the door before her nerves could talk her out of it and waited breathlessly. The door opened a few seconds later and standing in the doorway was well over six feet of gorgeous. His amazing eyes scanned her from head to toe before backing up and holding the door open for her to enter. As she passed by him she noticed the bottle of liquor in his hand and an empty hotel room. The two of them were alone.

"I'm in the safety of my hotel and don't plan to leave so there was no need to come and *check* on me, Carla," he said. "I'm a grown man..."

"I know that... I just," she tried.

Unwilling or, perhaps with help from the liquor, unable to help ease her discomfort, he instead stood there. Greg stared at her for the longest two minutes of her life. He was waiting for an explanation and she owed him that much but the desperation that had brought her here was losing to the fear that was keeping her from the whole purpose in coming.

Eying the liquid courage in his hand she instead said, "May I have a small bit of that?"

Glancing down at his hand holding the bottle he held it out to her and said, "The housekeeping staff forgot to leave any glasses... plastic or otherwise."

Past the point of caring, she took the bottle from his hand and took a drink of it. This wasn't exactly how she'd expected this night to go when she'd left the gallery. Doug had always been so good at reining her in and keeping her from running on nothing but her emotions.

Greg on the other hand seemed content to stand and watch her drinking hard liquor from a bottle almost like he was again *encouraging* her or daring her. She wasn't sure which. Did she have the guts to make the first move?

"I'm sorry for what I said to you. I didn't mean it. I just didn't want Meredith to know that I'm not... the perfect mother and wife that she thinks I am. Come to find out she's known that, since ninth grade at least, and was much less upset than I expected her to be," she blurted and then took another drink for more courage.

He walked over and sat on the edge of the large bed off to one side of the room and looked at her as if inviting her to continue. It had been a good while since she'd had anything stronger than a glass of wine and the couple of long swigs she'd taken from the bottle left her a little unsteady on the unusually high heels she wore.

She ungracefully stepped out of the shoes and felt his hazel eyes caress her legs as she bent to pick them up and hold them in her other hand which now held her wrap, her clutch and the shoes.

Forcing herself to meet his eyes, she lost the battle with herself to remain strong, say what she'd come to say, and then leave the next move up to him, when his beautiful lips curved up in a lopsided smile.

"Did you want to sit down, Carla?" he asked.

How could she meet his gaze when that mouth had solicited an excitement in her that she still felt several hours later from when they'd last made contact with her skin? Did he know that's what she was thinking about right now? Was that what was behind his grin?

Her knees grew weak so she moved forward and sat down a little heavier than she would have liked on the edge of his bed. Seeing that his beautiful lips still smiled down at her, she again took another long drink from the bottle. She would be drunk soon at this rate… courage not stupidity was what she was after.

"I sometimes let my emotions get the better of me… even the bad ones," she said, handing him the bottle. "That's no excuse for being so hateful toward you at the gallery, earlier. I realize now you… you will always be a cop. It's who you are and I'm sorry."

His eyes never left her as he also took a drink from the bottle and then offered it back to her before saying, "Is that all you see when you look at me, Carla? *A cop?*"

How could she answer that? Taking the bottle from his hand she again took another drink. Yes, she saw a cop when she looked at him but she also saw a man with amazing eyes, a good heart and that *mouth*.

Reaching across her body he took the bottle back out of her hand and she caught the smell of the cologne he always wore and the liquid courage took that opportunity to finally kick in.

Leaning forward, she pressed her mouth against his before he could pull back away from her. His mouth was incredibly soft for a man and it felt so good against hers. A soft kiss was all she got before he moved back from her. He stood up and took the bottle over to the desk and set it down. Then he came back and sat down next to her and said, "If all you see is the cop, then you shouldn't be kissing me."

"It's not all I see..." she supplied.

"*Then what?* Tell me what you see when you look at me, Carla? Do you see a cop, a man, a friend or just a reminder of how much you miss your husband?" he asked.

The liquor hadn't just given her courage, it was making her speak before she could even process what he asked and formulate a proper response because she heard herself say, "I know you were at the premiere with your... *friend*... but I didn't like that. As much as I miss Doug, I know he doesn't want me to be alone anymore. My only experience with the police was when they arrested me twenty five years ago. You're not like those cops were though."

"How were those cops? Were they mean to you?" he asked.

"No, they put handcuffs on me and it wasn't *my fault*... it was all Jarod. I told them I didn't know about the tickets being fakes... and I *didn't*... but they put the handcuffs on me anyways," she replied, remembering that night long ago and putting her hands together in front of her and looking at her wrists.

Reaching out, Greg took her hands and clasped them together and used one of his larger hands like a cuff to hold her hands in her lap then said, "Trina and I dated a long time ago for about thirty seconds. Now we are just friends... she's the sister of my old boss who asked if I would take her to the premiere tonight. She's dating someone else now but is really into art." After a short pause he continued, "What else do you see when you look at me, Carla?"

"I see your mouth in my dreams, kissing my skin... like earlier... making me *feel* like..." she blurted and then clamped her lips closed.

"What does my mouth make you feel like, Carla?" he asked, moving closer to her. *Just one more kiss from him and then she should go.*

"Like..." she said as he moved even closer. "Like a *woman*... not just a mother."

He leaned down close to her and pressed his lips against hers again. She struggled to free her hands from his grasp and wrap them around his neck but he wouldn't release her. The kiss was making her belly flutter as he touched his tongue to hers.

After a moment he released her mouth and leaned his forehead against hers whispering, "Do you want to know what I see when I look at you?"

Did she want to know? She did not compare with *Barbie* in any way and if that was the type of woman he was used to dating, he had to be sorely disappointed with her or at least he would be.

"I see a woman who cries as often as she laughs. I see a woman who puts everyone around her first. So much so that she feels guilty for even *considering* doing something small for herself, let alone something big like continuing her education. I see a beautiful emotional soul who shivers when I touch her because she feels things so deeply," he finished with his lips against hers.

Every hair on her body was standing up straight and she was surrounded by an electrical current that jumped from her to him as he kissed her again. He continued to hold her hands together in her lap with one of his but used his other hand to run his fingers through her hair and caress her neck. When he finally broke the kiss and pulled back from her it was to stare at her.

"Is that all you see when you look at me?" she asked nervously after seeing his piercing gaze strip her bare as though he knew her legs were jelly and her stomach a ball of sexual tension.

He kissed her a little more forcefully then and when he released her said, "I also see a woman who caught my attention from the first time we met. I stepped up close to you to look at one of Chuck's paintings and you looked up at me just like this and your lips parted as though inviting me to taste them. I see a woman whose touch sets my body on fire like nothing I've ever experienced before… so much so that she reduces me to *begging* for her touch. I see a woman who I want to make love to a little more every time I catch her staring at my mouth. I see the first woman in my life that I am still willing to wait for."

"You don't have to wait anymore… I told you… I know that Doug would want me to be happy and move on with my life. I noticed you that day too but I wasn't anywhere near ready for that yet. You've helped me with that process and I thank you for it. Now when I look at you, I just want to touch you so badly," she said, trying to pull her hands free.

"I'll let your hands go if you promise not to take over and just do this for me too. Again, I'm not a child… I'm a grown man who is *going* to participate in this, Carla," he said.

Chapter Ten

He was normally a good judge of people and could easily predict how they would react in certain situations. Carla, though, always did the unexpected. Where she was normally shy, emotional and could easily allow others to trample all over her, releasing her hands and then trying to take back some control again was like trying to catch a bird.

A part of him had known she would want to take care of the growing inferno between them, just like she took care of everything else in her life, but he was wholly unprepared for her level of sensuality.

Once her hands were free she leaned forward and began kissing him. She never released his mouth while managing to stand back up and move in front of him. She began undoing his tie and then the buttons of his shirt.

Those dainty hands on his shoulders and chest felt absolutely amazing. He realized he was in trouble long before she made it to the button of his pants. The onslaught of pleasure he felt knowing she finally wanted him only stopped by catching one of her hands in his.

The tables were turned on him yet again when she flipped her hand in his so that she was once more in control guiding his hand up the inside of one of her sexy thighs. Breaking her kiss for a moment she said the one thing that he hadn't anticipated.

"Mmmm, touch me, Greg. I want your hands and mouth on me," she said quietly as she guided his hand even higher under her dress.

Her breathing hitched as his hand cupped her cleft overtop of her panties. Standing before him he watched her head fall back on her shoulders while her hands tried to guide his shirt further down his arms.

He rubbed his hand along the silken material of her panties. The one barrier between his fingers and paradise. That scrap of material was the only thing keeping him from absolutely ravishing her right now. How could she expect him to make love to her when she was making him practically froth at the mouth?

In order to get his shirt all the way off he was forced to release her. She slid the shirt off one of his arms and then the other in such a way that she brushed up against his entire body and ensured that he could smell and practically taste her.

He tried to think of baseball or anything that would take his mind of the seduction of a professional. *God... she was so damn hot!* She deserved tenderness but if he didn't get control of this situation...

One would have expected her to properly fold or lay his shirt across a chair. Instead she tossed it carelessly on the floor. Then she leaned forward to rub her mouth across his shoulder as he had done to her earlier. She released noises of satisfaction that made him so hard he actually hurt. The moan escaped him before his hands made it back to her waist.

He wanted to try and pull her away from him. For just a minute so he could breathe and get himself in check. Again she did what he wouldn't have expected. She guided his hands up the outside of those soft shapely legs of hers. Dragging the hem of her dress up around her middle and only stopping when his hands were on either side of her hips.

This was what the phrase about a tiger in the bedroom was referring to. It was coined specifically for Carla Johnson. Her appetite for him was eating him alive but he was loving every second of it.

Hooking his thumbs under the flimsy string of material along each of her hips, he slowly pulled her panties down her thighs. She looked down at him. Her mouth parted softly and her bottom lip quivered. "I'm so wet…"she gasped before her head fell back on her shoulders once more.

All sense of decency escaped him at hearing something like that come from the normally prim and proper woman. He pushed her panties the rest of the way down her thighs a little rougher than he should have. Then he caressed her thighs, hips and waist as his hands slid back up her body taking the dress with it until she was standing before him gloriously naked.

"Take your pants off," she ordered.

"Maybe we should…" he offered. He was so unusually out of control with desire for her that he actually feared hurting her in his current state.

"No… now, Detective," she said breathlessly reaching shamelessly for the waistband of his pants. "I need you so bad right now I can't stand it… please… pleasure me."

In an effort to buy him some time to cope with her onslaught of blazing desire, he reached out and gently slid his fingers along her soft cleft. The wetness he was met with did not help his situation at all. Nor did the sharp gasp she emitted along with the words, "Oh God… yea."

"Carla… baby, you are tearing me up. I've wanted you so badly for so long and you pushed me away every time. Now you are making me crazy and this wasn't what I thought…" he tried to explain his feelings, but her soft, moist flesh against his hand wanted him more than it wanted an explanation.

Placing the small fingers of one hand on his mouth as though to shut him up, and pressing her other one over top his hand and pushing it firmly against the very core of her, she leaned down and whispered, "Harder, Greg…"

Thankfully he'd removed his shoes, socks and the belt of his trousers before she'd shown up at his door this evening or his next stunt wouldn't have been so successful. With his mostly useless left hand he finally unzipped his pants. Sitting forward he managed to stand up and push them down his legs along with his underwear while his other hand never left her weeping body. She was putting every dream he'd ever had of her to shame as her hips and body moved in time with his fingers.

As soon as he was naked and had kicked the last of his clothes aside, her free hand found him. She wrapped her hand around his shaft just perfectly and he suddenly couldn't breathe at all.

Gasping for air, he felt like he was drowning. When she stepped up close to him and kissed him so hungrily he found himself clutching her by the time she released him. He was unbalanced as all the blood rushed to the place that her talented hand now stroked as though she'd practiced making his body sing a song just for her a thousand times before.

"I'm dizzy, Carla," he whispered against her mouth. "I want you worse than I've ever wanted anything in my whole life. Please... stop tormenting me with your beautiful body and talented hands... put me out of my misery."

She released her hold on his overheated and excited body. Her hands stroked up his stomach to his chest which she gently pushed on until he was forced to sit back down on the bed. Giving him no reprieve from the skill she possessed at loving a man she followed him onto the bed, straddling his hips just as he felt her clench around his fingers. Unable to wait a second longer to possess her delicious heat he guided her hips down to him and nudged into her soft core. *Oh man, she felt amazing.*

"Carla... a condom... wallet," he managed to choke out when his sense of responsibility managed to fight through the fog of sensual tension racing throughout his whole body.

"I'm safe and can't have any more babies now," she whispered against the side of his neck achieving what he thought was impossible... making him even harder.

"Good, I'm safe too," he whispered as he tried to catch her mouth with his when she gently bit his neck and then backed up to look in his eyes.

Her gaze went straight to his mouth and again he tried to lean forward and kiss her lips. Instead of letting him, she backed up and shifted her hips which slid the last of him into her beautiful body. She rocked her hips against him and the pleasure of it had him groaning her name loudly.

"You're big and you feel so good to me," she told his mouth before her gaze finally met his again. Her hips found a rhythm that continued to bring him to the brink and then force him back from the ledge over and over again.

"Please, Carla. God, what are you doing to me?" he managed to say before his head fell back on his shoulders.

"I'm touching you, Greg Sanders... just like you ask me to," she said before sucking the skin of his neck into her sweet mouth. "Do you like it?"

"Shit... yea. I fucking love it," he gasped as she worked him over.

At his breathless admission she leaned her whole body back from his. She began moving faster and harder against him until she cried out in a husky voice that shot straight to his groin. The feel of her clenching tightly around him finally allowed him to slip over the edge of sanity into complete ecstasy. He cried out another admission as his body emptied into hers, "I love you, Carla."

The words were out and he couldn't take them back. *Hell...* he didn't want to take them back. For a man who had once said he would never get married or have kids, he was completely and totally in love with a woman who had three... make that four kids. He managed to sit forward slightly so that he could wrap his left arm around her as well, rather than using it as leverage now that she was done with him.

He was enjoying the feel of her snuggled against him almost as much as he'd enjoyed her version of touching him. She'd just ruined him for any other woman. No other woman had ever satisfied him like she just did or ever stood a chance of being able to. The loss of her skin against his was almost painful when she pulled back from him.

"Oh... I'm so sorry... did I hurt your shoulder?" she asked.

Finally able to catch her off guard he leaned forward and caught her mouth in a series of heated open mouth kisses that left his body wanting her again... and maybe again after *that*. Damn... he just wanted her... heart, body and soul! *Night and day... always... forever.*

"Did you hear me, Carla?" he said between kisses. "I love you, beautiful... I don't want to be without you anymore. I'm not trying to replace Doug or what he meant to you. I would never do that to you... but damn it... I'm so in love with you. Please... say something."

He watched as her eyes filled up with those tears that left him grasping at anything that would make them stop. Then she said, "I never thought I would feel like this again after Doug died. I was so afraid to allow what was happening between us to come to fruition... in case something happened to you too. I still am afraid of that. I mean you got shot for heaven's sake!"

With her declaration she released him from the sweet warmth nestled between her legs. She got off the bed and headed into the bathroom, closing the door behind her. He wanted to follow her but he also didn't want to push her too far... especially now.

Being with her had changed everything for him. Somehow in his heart he'd known making love with her would seal his fate. She had drawn him in from the first time he'd laid eyes on her and hadn't let him go since. Now he didn't want to let her go either.

Laying back on the bed for fear his shaking legs wouldn't hold him if he stood up, he listened to the shower start up. Carla had done all the work and it had felt so good... he was satisfied but wanted more. She hadn't said she loved him in return but she hadn't just left either.

Right now she was in his territory and like a dog he intended to mark her as his own before she left this room. He wanted something concrete that told anyone who looked at her that she belonged to him.

Getting up he went to the door of the bathroom and knocked. He opened the door and went inside when she advised him that she was in the shower. Stepping into the shower behind her, he stood and stared at her until he couldn't take it anymore.

"Turn around, Carla," he said.

She turned around slowly and met his gaze. A temptation was what she was. As if challenging him, he watched her suck on her bottom lip as her hand slid down her stomach and further still to the small patch of hair that hid her sex.

There had been other women in his past that had tried to use sex against him, but Carla was better at it… experience made all the difference. She used it to distract him and make him lose focus.

He came in here to seduce *her* this time… to try and extract the words he wanted to hear from her. Now all he could do was watch her silent way of reminding him just how good she felt as well as how much he adored her.

Never again would he be able to look at her and just see a soft hearted mother who tugged at his heart strings. Along with that he would see a sexy siren that could very easily chain him like a dog and lead him around on a very short leash.

"I want to know… need to know… how you feel about me, Carla," he said.

Then in awe he watched as her free hand made its way back up her wet body to her breasts and her head fell back. She was going to kill him with this. No more… he was letting her make him come undone just from watching her instead of having the conversation he needed to have.

"I'm serious," he said, trying to ignore how effectively she was manipulating his body as well as his mind.

"Me too…" she whispered.

Then she pulled the shower curtain open and got out closing it back shut behind her. He stuck his head under the spray of the water, willing the image of her away. Sometime later when he finished his own shower and exited the bathroom, he came up short at seeing her in his bed, hugging one of the pillows, her temptingly naked back on display... *sleeping*. He wanted to scream his frustration to the wind.

She had finally allowed him to be with her. While it had been wonderful it had done little to ease his need for her... it had simply shifted it. Now he needed her to feel the same way about him that he felt about her. However, if sleeping kept her here with him for the night, he would take it. Decision made, he crawled in beside her and after she released the pillow one thin arm immediately draped across his chest. She curled into a smaller ball pressing her face and lips against his rib cage.

Like a glove, she fit in the curve of his side perfectly and he found himself jealous of a dead man. Had Doug Johnson known what a gem he'd married all those years ago? Somehow Greg knew the man probably did and only prayed that he too would be given an equal chance to make her happy. Her satisfied sigh told him perhaps he was off to a good start.

Greg awoke to the sounds of someone whimpering. Opening his eyes he found Carla lying next to him with her eyes tightly shut. One slender arm stuck out from beneath the blanket on the bed and was trying to hold as much of her forehead as possible. *Hangover*.

He gently got out of the bed, pulled on his underwear and then dug in his suitcase until he unearthed his first aid kit and took out a packet of aspirin. Remembering that there weren't any cups in his room, he walked over and picked up the bottle of liquor.

After dumping what was left of the liquor out of the bottle, he rinsed it and filled it with water from the bathroom. Then he headed back to his side of the bed and sat on the edge. Leaning down he kissed one bare shoulder and whispered, "Sit up, beautiful."

In typical Carla style, always doing the last thing he expected, she did exactly what he told her to and sat up. Rather than being shy around him after introducing him to the most amazing sex of his entire life, she simply allowed the stark white sheet to fall to her waist.

It took him a moment to remember his purpose but he eventually tore the packet of aspirin open with his teeth. She squinted at him but held out her hand. She put the pills in her mouth and reached for a drink but upon seeing the liquor bottle she adamantly shook her head no.

"No... it's water... I dumped out what was left," he said and handed it to her.

She took a drink, winced and then took another drink before handing the bottle back to him. He sat it on the night stand and turned back to her. Seeing the heel of her hand pushed against her forehead as though pushing back against the pain, he fluffed his pillows and leaned back. Then he pulled her by her shoulder to lay her head on his chest and stomach. He managed pull the sheet back over her which was more for his benefit than hers. He wanted her again... *badly*.

Instead he allowed her to use him as a pillow while he combed his fingers through her short but soft hair. It was nice being here like this with her and aside from hating that she was in pain, he enjoyed holding her this way. He was normally out and gone the morning after... even during his serious relationships. It had always felt uncomfortable... like they were expecting something from him he either wasn't able or willing to give. Carla didn't need or want anything from him... except for pleasure and even with that she'd given more than she received.

"That feels good," she whispered against his stomach after some time had passed, "But I should go... Meredith or Chuck will come to check on me and if I'm not in my room..."

"When can I see you again?" he asked.

"We leave to go home tomorrow so..." she replied. "I'd love to see you from time to time... whenever you happen to be in Florida visiting Becca or whatever. It's doubtful I'll be able to make it back up here anytime soon, with the boys and all but I hope you'll at least keep in touch."

Stay in touch? That was on the low scale of what he wanted from her. Perhaps it was the effects of the morning after but he'd had plenty of experience in this area and never before had it left him with stars in his eyes and a feeling like *love* in his heart. Carla Johnson had changed his whole outlook on relationships and she merely wanted him to stay in touch.

As if the cat had his tongue and was threatening his very sanity, he lay there watching as she got up out of his bed, ran a hand through her short hair and then pulled on her panties and eventually her dress. Bringing up his slip about how strong his feelings were for her the night before, didn't seem like a good idea at the moment. Damn if he didn't want to be with her just as badly, if not worse, now that he'd enjoyed her, as when the idea of making love to her was a mere fantasy. He had it bad for her but this time was different… he was desperate for her to return his feelings.

She approached him, with her high heel shoes dangling from one hand and bent to kiss him. It felt like a goodbye kiss and his heart couldn't take it after having waited all these months for her heart to open up and give him a chance. Sitting up he caught her head in between his hands and brought her mouth to his several more times. If a person could speak using no words at all, then he hoped her heart somehow heard what he was saying.

Instead she quietly gathered the remainder of her belongings and left his room. He lay there for several minutes replaying the events of last evening and wondering how in such a short time, after years of denial, he'd gone from being an advocate for bachelorhood, to being willing to sell his soul for a chance at something more with her.

After showering he called Becca. His sister was a force to be reckoned with, especially now that Dickie had helped bring her inner spirit to the surface.

"They already know… so I cannot run interference for you two while she sneaks back to her room," Becca answered with a laugh. "All I ask is that you be careful with her… don't hurt her. She means a lot to Chuck… to the whole group. Especially with the way she has taken Chuck under her wing and no one wants to see her get hurt."

"She's not the one who is going to be hurt," he muttered into the phone.

"Oh, I see…" Becca replied quietly. "I was really hoping that something would happen between you two but perhaps I was reading signs that weren't there?"

"It's no secret, Becca. You know me better than anyone… I *really* like her. Who am I kidding? I've got it bad for her… I think I have since I went to her house with you that first time," he said. "I think maybe my desire for her maybe just pushed her to far too fast. Maybe I just need to give her some space to think about what if any feelings she *does* have for me."

"Yea... I know. Dickie has been nothing but patient with me and I couldn't love him more for it. Carla seems to want to be everything to everyone... especially her kids... so much so that she sometimes almost waits too long to act on things *she* wants or needs," Becca said. "My tip for the day is that this time you may have to fight for what you want. Unlike the women in your past... Carla is unlikely to simper at your feet and beg for your attention. She has a family and responsibilities that will come first and will *always* take precedence over any feelings she may have for you. You are going to have to show her that you can fit into her life in order for her to make room for you in it. Sorry to say this, but you aren't going to be able to do that from here in New York."

"What are you saying?" he asked.

"I'm saying that you need to close up your apartment, come back down to Florida and prove your worth to her. Support her, be there for her... make yourself invaluable to her... you can stay at the beach house for as long as you need," Becca replied. "She has feelings for you but you're going to have to coax them out of her a little bit."

Hanging up with Becca, he thought about what she'd said. Family was everything to Carla while he knew next to nothing about having a family. *Could he be a family man?* Wanting to be with her was one thing but *could* he fit into her world?

Chuck and Meredith obviously approved but they were adults. He'd never even contemplated having kids, let alone voluntarily being involved with them. All he could do was try but Becca was right that he couldn't do that from here in New York. If that's what he had to do to wake up with Carla *everyday*... he'd do it. After all she hadn't said she *didn't* love him in return.

After showering and getting dressed, he headed for his apartment. He had a million things to do if he expected to return to Florida for an unspecified amount of time. Making sure that Jarrod Tompkins would remain behind bars for a while was at the top of that list. One area that could help him fit in was keeping them all safe.

Just as he was about to call the sergeant and get an update on the case, his cell phone rang. Seeing Rusty Hawkins' number on his caller ID he accepted the call.

"Hey, buddy. I thought I'd call and see if finding out where about ninety percent of all that money went would help?" Rusty asked when he answered.

"Wow, that was fast. I can see being deployed hasn't caused you to lose your edge any. You should consider getting into law enforcement once you do actually get out of the service," he replied.

"Hell no... I'm done carrying a gun unless it's for hunting. I don't think I can do it anymore to be honest. I emailed you the information that I found. Pass it onto your guys on the force but I'd appreciate it if you cleaned my name off of it first," Rusty said.

"Sure... and I owe you one," he replied.

"Nah… you don't owe me anything but after I get out… if you're ever in Ohio stop in and say, 'hi'. It's been a while and we need to catch up. Maybe I can introduce you to a few of my friends from the service," Rusty said.

"Looking forward to it," he replied before hanging up.

After closing up his apartment properly Greg advised the landlord that he would be out of town on an extended trip. Then stopping at the post office he had his mail forwarded to Becca's beach house, before finally calling the Sheriff's Office.

Greg felt better after hearing about the charges leveled at Jarrod and being assured that he wouldn't be making bail anytime soon considering the dollar amount involved. He also managed to sweet talk his buddy into emailing him a list of victims after explaining that Chuck intended to try and make their loss a little easier to take.

Having done all he could and knowing it was really late he headed back to the hotel where he found the men of the group gathered in the lounge of the bar talking loudly, laughing, planning the event for the victims of Jarrod's scam and having a good time. Greg had friends… plenty of friends. Rusty being one of his closest ones, but this group... they felt like his people… family. He finally understood what drew Becca to them. It felt like he had known every one of them for decades.

He was really starting to enjoy himself along with the drink he'd ordered when the conversation turned to the women of the group. Looking over at him, Bobby Jackson said, "So now that you're back in the saddle so to speak… thanks to *Carla*… you ready to learn to ride a motorcycle too?"

The guys all laughed when he nearly choked to death on the whiskey he'd taken a drink of. He only managed a nod of his head.

"Good… Dickie can help you with a seat for it and then it's all ready to roll. We got the Arizona ride coming up in a few months. I'm thinking you are going to want to ride with us and not be stuck riding in the campers with the women and kids," he said with a laugh and smack to Greg's back that made him laugh too. "Never pictured hitting the road with a retired *cop* but I'll make an exception for you. Besides… I like donuts too."

The guys all laughed as if they had just accepted him into the fold and given him their stamp of approval on pursuing Carla. Now if he could just get her to agree to something more than simply keeping in touch.

Chapter Eleven

The two weeks after returning from New York were even busier than normal. Chuck had taken to working non-stop on the painting he planned to give away at the event for those people who had been victimized by Jarrod. Meredith had been working with both Dana and Lilly on planning the event and finalizing wedding plans. Carla had managed to get the boys back into a school routine just in time for orientation at the college and for classes to start.

She must be insane to try and cram in college courses on top of everything else that was going on. Greg had talked her into this but he wasn't the one having to worry about lining up babysitters for the boys, planning meals for them on the nights she wouldn't be around, finding someone to help them with homework when she was at class and above all trying not to completely disrupt their lives. Amazingly, instead of staying in New York, Greg had come back down to Florida with the group and started working part time at the motorcycle shop that Bobby Jackson owned.

The crazy group of bikers had enfolded Greg into their midst like he was one of their own, much to her chagrin. Now he was around every corner she turned, or at least that's how it felt. This made putting the amazing night she'd spent in his arms behind her nearly impossible.

She had meant what she said about seeing him from time to time, but that had been meant as more of a tension reliever… a way of enjoying their time together and then getting back to her regularly scheduled life, than the truth. It was her way of saying goodbye.

Instead of just being faced with memories of him at night, she was slapped with them on a daily basis. Somehow he became more gorgeous each time she saw him, as though he was more than ten years younger than he really was.

His sinful mouth was constantly grinning at her in such a way as to whisper memories of how good it had felt on her skin. Combine that with catching his scent from time to time and it was nearly unbearable. He smelled like some amazingly rugged alpha male ensuring all other males in his territory knew him to be the one in charge. It set her body on fire and her nerves on edge.

At least he was being a gentleman about it and not constantly trying to get her back into his bed. She was a mother but she was also a woman and pleasure like Greg Sanders was capable of only reminded her of that fact.

Carla recognized her own weakness and was no longer strong enough to resist him now that she knew his taste, his smell, and the way he *felt*. The liquor she'd consumed that night had helped take the edge off of her nerves over being with a different man after more than twenty years with the same one. She had wondered if she could even go through with it but thinking her chance of being with him was either now or never had emboldened her.

Greg didn't share the same rugged looks as the rest of the guys who worked at Bobby Jackson's motorcycle shop. Somehow clean shaven and clean cut he still fit right in. He was just as much a dare devil as the rest of them seemed to be with no sense of propriety or dignity.

When she had stopped by on her way to college to drop off the lunch Chuck had left behind and let him know the boys would be picked up by her father, the group had been in the side alley teaching Greg to ride on a smaller dirt-bike.

Once it was obvious that Greg could handle the bike just fine, the *training* had quickly changed to a competition of sorts. Despite the fact that the bike was obviously too small for them, the guys were each taking a turn riding on it. The object of the game was apparently to see who could get to the end of the alley the fastest.

Knowing they were unaware that she had pulled up in front of the garage bay, she remained in the safety of her car and simply watched them all. It was like watching grade school children who weren't being properly supervised.

They were laughing and giving each other a hard time as they each took a turn speeding down the alleyway on the small bike with their knees up near their elbows. When that no longer held the same appeal they quickly adjusted to trying to ride wheelies instead.

Though she should probably get out and put a stop to their fun before one of them really hurt themselves, she couldn't shake the smile on her face at their antics. The mischievous smile Greg wore was simply breathtaking and drew her gaze like a moth to a flame.

After a few close calls she expected they would call it quits but instead it only seemed to make them more determined to keep the bike on one wheel for the entire length of the alley. Glancing around it appeared that Lilly Jackson wasn't working at the moment, which explained a lot.

After Tommy McMurray rode a little too close to the wall of the building resulting in torn jeans, she figured it was time to make her presence known. Getting out, she approached the group who stood around talking and laughing.

The entire group jumped and turned around quickly to face her when she held up Chuck's lunch and said, "Did you forget something, Chuck?"

They each shared a look of guilt over having been caught, including Bobby Jackson who attempted to shield the dirt bike with his body as though she hadn't already spent ten minutes watching what they were doing.

Greg granted her a smile coated with images of sin that must have come from the devil himself. Then he stepped up way too close to her and took the lunch she held from her hand. God help but her eyes went straight to her favorite part of the man and his sexy grin only widened.

Tommy McMurray smacking Chuck on the back of his head while Greg held the lunch out to Chuck was the only thing that made her remember where she was... dragging her back from memories of that mouth.

Heading back to her car, she knew they were all watching her walk away but the only stare she cared about was the one she could *feel* coming from the most amazing hazel eyes. She couldn't even look at him as she managed to back out and drive away. Half way to the campus she realized what the group of women saw in these men... they were fun and none of them took themselves or their lives too seriously.

This included Greg for the most part and that was what bothered her the most. Yes, the arrogance they displayed as though shaking their fists at fate was captivating and sexy as hell, but life wasn't a guarantee. In an instant it could be over and none of them seemed to even care!

Her afternoon was spent touring the campus with a nice young man around Chuck's age and that only served to make her nervous that she would in fact be the oldest adult at the college. She then stopped at the bookstore and picked up the last book she needed for her classes, just in time to make it to her first class.

When the session ended she sat for several minutes looking through the materials the professor had handed out as well as her syllabus and the book. Stuffing all the information into her bag, she took out her cell phone. Upon seeing the time, she hurried home.

Pulling up out front she was surprised to find Gretchen McMurray and the boys in the side yard. Gretchen's hands were crossed over her chest and she was burning Ben a dirty look. Matt stood between the two of them as though running interference, holding a football in his hands.

Parking the car, she looked around and realized that while Meredith's car was gone, as was Chuck's bike, Greg Sanders' car was parked out in front of the house. *What was going on now?*

Getting out of the car she heard Gretchen say, "Because I said so, Ben!"

"You're not the boss, Gretchen! I am... I'm the quarterback! Mr. Sanders said so..." Ben replied. "Besides... girls don't play football as a job!"

"Are we going to play? Stop being bossy, Gretchen and, Ben, we can all be the quarterback... we can just take turns," Matt explained.

Sometimes it was hard not to interfere when the three of them played together. While Matt was quite a bit taller than Gretchen, he had a thin build taking more after her than Doug. Ben on the other hand was *all* Doug and nearly as tall as Matt but with a husky build. He was nearly twice the size of the little girl.

Gretchen didn't let her small size stop her. She held her own just fine and won as often as she lost her arguments with Ben and Matt. So rather than getting involved in their childhood spat, she headed inside to find out what was going on.

As Carla made her way into the kitchen she stopped and stared in shock. Greg Sanders had baby Melody strapped to his chest in a child carrier. The baby was squealing in delight as her thin little arms and legs kicked a mile a minute. The baby had so many medical and developmental issues most of the group treated her with delicate gloves.

Greg obviously having no experience with children, especially babies, and must not have noticed this. So rather than facing his chest as Melody normally did with her parents, she was facing outward. Something about the whole scene gave her pause so she just watched and waited.

For the first time perhaps ever, the baby looked and acted her age. As Greg brought a potato chip to his mouth, Melody reached out and grabbed his hand as though to take the chip from him and then watched the progress his hand made to his mouth.

Carla had never been so grateful to have three healthy children as she was when she spent any time around Melody. One wouldn't know there was any difference at all between this baby and another at the moment.

"Not a chance, *girlfriend*. Chips will make you fat," Greg told the baby before putting the chip in his own mouth. "I'm a cop but not a *mean* one so I won't make you eat that crap. I got some instant mashed potatoes for you instead… but no chips."

Stepping back around the doorway so she was less likely to be noticed, she continued to watch him. Would he really feed the baby table food rather than the jar of baby food that set on the counter opened with a baby spoon sticking out of it? Melody was old enough to try some table food, at least by Carla's estimation but Tommy and Dana constantly worried about her being so small and therefore followed the nutrition recommendations fully.

Even with a flailing infant strapped to his chest and what looked like dried baby food... *carrots*... smeared down the side of his shirt, Greg Sanders was still one of the sexiest men she'd ever seen.

He took the baby spoon out the carrots and rinsed it off saying, "I know... it gags me too."

Then he dipped the spoon into a small bowl of mashed potatoes sitting on the counter and took a bite of it. After swallowing his bite he said, "Yea, that's more like it. Forgive me for not realizing that your parents packed *gruel* for you to eat."

With that he dipped the spoon and scooped some more mashed potatoes onto it. Bending around awkwardly to see Melody's face he spooned it into her open mouth. *So much for not sharing germs.* Melody obviously liked what she'd eaten and turned her head to look up at Greg after eating the bite and fussed as though impatient for the next. Carla watched him feed the baby. He was grinning like a clown the whole time until the buzzer on the oven went off.

"No pizza either... mashed potatoes is all you get," Greg advised the baby.

As soon as he was no longer spooning the food into her mouth, the baby began to fuss as he turned off the timer and the oven. Deciding he could use some help, Carla stepped out from her hiding place and said, "Here, I can get the pizza... I think someone is ready for another bite."

"Busted... twice in one day! That must be a new record," Greg said to Melody before scooping up another spoonful of mashed potatoes from the bowl.

After pulling the pizza out of the oven she turned back to him and watched for a few more moments as he continued to shovel food into the baby's mouth, stopping periodically to give her a drink from a regular cup.

Carla could only hope what she was seeing in the cup was formula and not regular milk, since the canister of formula set next to the cup along with a spoon that very possibly was used to stir the formula. He was making a complete mess and was obviously clueless about what he was doing but his improvising skills were commendable.

"Before you ask... there was only one bottle in the bag and after that was empty I realized you don't have a brush thingy to clean it with so I just mixed up some more in this. Besides... shouldn't she be drinking from a regular cup by now anyways?" he asked.

At only eight months old... some babies might be ready for a Sippy cup but this baby was not nearly ready for that, let alone a regular cup. Realizing he was looking for reassurance she simply smiled and said, "You're doing fine."

"I sent the other kids outside to play. That's what my grandpa always did with Becca and me when he needed to make dinner," he volunteered as though needing to explain his actions when all she really wanted to know was why he'd been left alone with all four children.

"They were playing just fine when I came inside," she offered.

"Good... I *told* Dana I could handle it. She didn't look convinced but now I have a witness. None of them were harmed while in my care," he said finally, looking away from Melody and over to her.

"Dana dropped them off here?" she asked incredulously. Dana was the most responsible person she'd ever met. So for her to just drop her children off meant something must be terribly wrong.

"Lilly Jackson went into labor. Chuck and Meredith are somewhere tasting cake or some such. Tommy took a bike to drop off to a customer and Dickie and Becca took the girls to Tampa for the weekend since they don't have school tomorrow. Dana said she needed to get Edna Jackson to the hospital to be with Bobby and Lilly, plus Dana's a labor coach... whatever that means. So anyways, she stopped by with the girls and when she found out you weren't here... I offered to watch em' instead and yea... I'm making a big mess. This is harder than I thought it would be," he finished, throwing his hands up as though in defeat.

Seeing that he was definitely in over his head and had obviously taken on more than he could chew in an effort to help out a friend, she stepped forward and put her hand on his arm.

"I'm pretty sure that's the most I've ever seen this baby eat. Why don't I take her and get her cleaned up and situated while you call the kids in and feed them some pizza and chips. There are juice boxes for them in the fridge," she offered.

Melody fussed when Carla finally managed to get her out of the carrier and actually reached for Greg. Seeing it as opportunity to re-emphasize that he was doing a good job with them she said, "Well I guess maybe we should trade jobs?"

Greg removed the empty carrier from his chest and then took Melody back from her. The baby unabashedly smiled at him and squealed. She could relate to that feeling. It was hard to look at the man and not giggle... he was just so good looking. Finding the wet wipes in the diaper bag, she opened them and set them on the counter near Greg before heading back outside to call the kids in.

Seeing that life at her house had carried on just fine while she'd been at class made her smile... especially since instead of Meredith or even her father who'd taken charge it had been *Detective Sanders*. Stepping into the backyard she was shocked to find Gretchen McMurray straddling Ben who lay on his back on the ground still holding the football.

"I said it was my turn now, Bennie... now give me that damn football!" Gretchen yelled a mere inch from Ben's face.

Instead of crying or being angry, her youngest lay there laughing only to stop long enough to say, "Make me you scrawny shrimp!"

Seeing the look of pure anger that passed the little girl's face, she hurried over to them and gently pulled Gretchen off of Ben just as Matt said, "I told them to stop it, Mom."

After making the two youngest kids apologize to each other Carla herded them all inside. Tommy McMurray arrived to pick up the girls just as she'd managed to change Melody's diaper and re-pack things into the diaper bag. Where twenty minutes earlier her boys and Gretchen had been fighting like siblings... now they all three looked annoyed that Gretchen had to leave to go home.

"I'm so sorry about this... I should have known from personal experience that babies often decide to make their grand appearance at the most inconvenient times. I got here as soon as I could," Tommy said.

"No worries... any news on the baby yet?" she asked him.

"No. Dana says Lilly's taking it like a champ but Bobby... not so much," he laughed.

"You should've stopped off and checked on him before you worried about the girls, they're fine here," she replied.

"I know but Dana wasn't sure since you weren't home," Tommy replied, looking skeptically at Greg.

"Just like learning how to control a motorcycle... I pick things up quick... you didn't need to worry," Greg laughed.

"The girls are just fine if you want to run to the hospital and see how Bobby's holding up. Besides, Edna might tire out and need to go home before the baby actually arrives," she suggested.

"Can't Gretchen just stay overnight with us, Mom? It's basically the weekend since there isn't school tomorrow," Matt asked.

"I'm sorry for what I said, Ms. Carla and I'll be real good from now on," Gretchen chimed in her agreement with Matt.

"Four kids is a lot for anyone to handle, Carla. Are you sure?" Tommy asked skeptically.

"I'll be here to help. I did get the baby to eat a pretty good amount this evening," Greg offered, obviously proud of his accomplishment.

"That's good to hear… she's been eating like a bird for days now," Tommy smiled.

"Instant mashed potatoes… she liked those a *whole* lot better than the carrots. That stuff smelled like it might be bad," Greg explained, making a face as though disgusted at the mere mention of the baby food.

Tommy laughed and then said, "I slip Melody real food too from time to time. I kind of feel bad for her but she's Dana's first baby. So I go along with it and slip her what I can, when Dana's not looking. My mom did it with me and I turned out okay and Gretchen *refused* to eat any of the baby food from the store from day one, but Dana's trying to do things by the book… so what can you do?"

"You go on and one of you can just come by in the morning and pick the girls up then. I have your numbers if we need anything. Go… be with your friends… they need you right now," Carla insisted.

"Yes!" she heard Ben whisper under his breath.

Once Tommy left for the hospital and the kids had finished eating, Greg sent them back outside with juice boxes and strict instructions not to go near the gate that led to the pool and to share the much sought after football. Matt was placed in charge as he was the oldest and the three of them took off for the side yard where they had been earlier.

Greg cleaned up the table while she situated the baby on the floor with some toys and then went to find blankets and pillows as well as pajamas for Gretchen to wear.

Soon enough she heard Chuck and Meredith downstairs talking to Greg in the kitchen. After Greg explained to them that Lilly was in labor and that he would be around to help out with the kids, the young couple took off back out the door in a rush to get to the hospital.

It was hard not to be excited about the new baby. The whole group was like one large extended family and a new member was always welcome.

After getting Matt's room set up for both of the boys so that Gretchen could use Ben's room, Carla went back downstairs to the kitchen where she found Greg holding Melody again while pointing out the other kids through the window. Upon seeing her enter the room he turned and grinned at her.

He had cleaned up the entire kitchen and looked content to watch Melody and the kids. She wasn't sure if she should feel guilty or what but she couldn't help but be impressed. The household had always been her domain.

She took care of the family and Doug had taken care of the bills. It was a little old fashioned but she wouldn't have changed a thing. It had worked well for them for more than twenty years.

Everything in her life had changed when Doug had died. Watching Greg talking softly to Melody who looked absolutely awestruck by him cleared the cobwebs from her mind. There had been a time when she had thought her own life was over… everything she knew and loved had died that night.

In its place was left heartache, grief and an overwhelming sense that she might grow old alone without Doug there. She could remember hitting her knees in church one Sunday praying that God would see her through the pain.

The storm clouds had since cleared and left behind an amazing young man with tattoos and a heart of gold that had stepped in and pulled her family back from the brink in more ways than one. Through Chuck she had then met a group of people who were *real* friends… not the kind of friends who had shown up at Doug's funeral and offered awkward words of condolence… but rather the kind who felt more like family and held you when you cried.

Then as an added bonus a blonde haired, hazel eyed man with the most kissable mouth had awakened her heart, body and soul that had been slowly slipping away. *If only he were a safe bet.* She'd thought Doug was a sure thing… he had *never* been a risk taker and yet he'd been stolen away from her in the blink of an eye.

Greg was the opposite of that… he was… *had been*… a cop that bad guys shot at and had now begun riding around on motorcycles. He was a bit of an adrenaline junky and Carla just couldn't allow herself to love like that again… especially a risk taker. Losing another man she loved would surely kill her… and Greg was a far cry from a safe bet.

"Your dad called… I told him what was going on and he said he would just call you tomorrow when things were a little more calm," Greg smiled.

Walking over to join Greg at the window, she watched as Gretchen threw the football as hard as her little muscles would allow while Ben caught it with hardly any effort at all.

"He's quite good, isn't he?" she finally admitted as she watched her youngest son.

"Yes… he is. I don't profess to know how well other kids his age play but he does seem to be a natural at it," Greg replied. "Maybe you should take Gretchen's advice and ask Dana about helping the boy with his school work."

"Did you ever want kids of your own?" she asked Greg.

"No… never did. I find I'm content helping other people with theirs," he said and winked at her.

It was nearly eleven thirty before the kids settled down upstairs and the baby fell asleep in a mobile bassinet that Chuck had brought back from Tommy and Dana's house before going back over to the hospital. Without a word… *or a kiss*… Greg had wished her a good night and then just left.

He had been such a huge help this evening that she felt a softness toward him in addition to her normal physical attraction. Perhaps along with not wanting kids of his own he wasn't cut out for dating a woman with kids either. *Better to know that now.*

She woke in the early morning hours to Melody humming contentedly in her bassinet. After changing her and feeding her a bottle, Melody fell back asleep but Carla was wide awake by then. Laying Melody back down in the bassinet, Carla went in search of her cell phone and found a text message from Chuck.

```
Robert Jackson III born at 3:33AM
weighs eight pounds and three ounces.
Mom and baby are healthy and happy.
Dad passed out like a big pussy lol.
Bobby might be a wuss but Lilly is bad
ass.  Edith and I will be at the
apartment since its closer.  We will be
home first thing in the morning.
```

Another Bobby Jackson. Edna Jackson would be thrilled and Carla looked forward to joining the group to celebrate the arrival of the little guy. She put some coffee on and when it was done, she checked on Melody then took her coffee cup out to the front porch to sit and say thanks. For all that had been taken from her, equal amounts had also been given. A little while later when she came back out with her second cup she was surprised to see Greg pulling into the driveway.

As Greg approached where she sat he smiled and then said, "Edna Jackson just called me and said that she cannot wait another single minute to see her new grandbaby. She went on to say she had called every last one of the 'boys' and no one was answering their phone and that she would make me a pie if I'd come give her a ride over to the hospital. I told her that I would send you over to get her since you're better at the baby thing than I am. Might want to hurry... I think she was a little serious about not waiting another minute. I'm here to feed the kids cereal and generally mess up your house."

An hour later Carla had Edna Jackson packed up in the car and as they drove toward the hospital the older woman patted her hand and said, "That Greg Sanders is a good man, Carla."

She only nodded her acknowledgment that he was, but then said, "Yea he is... he's just a little bit more perilous than I am cut out to handle. Being shot apparently wasn't enough for him... now he's going to ride a motorcycle with the rest of them too. *Dangerous*."

Edna smiled and said, "It's too bad we don't know, going in, how something will work out in the end." Then after a brief pause she continued, "But then again... wouldn't that take the fun and life out of the journey anyways? To know the ending before the beginning? I kind of feel like it's best to just enjoy the time you get with a person rather than worrying about how *long* you get with them. One breath at a time... or something like that."

Chapter Twelve

Greg checked in on the baby who was sleeping peacefully. Then in preparation of the three kids waking up he got out cereal, bowls, spoons and milk and set them on the counter. After climbing the stairs and finding Ben's room empty he headed down the hallway to Matt's room.

Opening the door, he found all three kids sleeping in a messy pile of blankets, pillows and toys... on the floor. The youngest and smallest of the group was in the middle of the two boys.

"You kids ready for breakfast?" he asked.

After a few seconds, Gretchen opened her eyes and sighing heavily said, "Boy do I need coffee-milk this morning."

He managed to get the kids settled at the bar with cereal and then mixed up baby cereal and fruit from a jar of baby food he found in the diaper bag, just as Melody woke up. The fruit wasn't near as bad as the carrots so he went and picked the baby up and headed back out to the kitchen wondering how he was going to get the baby stuffed into the pouch that Dana had said she liked so much. He needed both hands free to feed the child... one hand to spoon in the food and one to keep her grubby little hands from grabbing the utensil.

Holding her squirming little body in his good arm, he attempted to use his injured arm to loop the leg holes over the baby's legs, when Gretchen said, "What are you doing Mr. Sanders?"

"Trying to get your sister in her pouch so I can feed her some breakfast too," he replied.

"Why don't you just sit her in her car seat?" Gretchen asked.

Out of the mouths of babes. It was distressing that after twenty five years as a detective he hadn't thought to use the car seat to feed the baby and instead needed to have the obvious pointed out to him by a five year old little girl too smart for her own good. This realization was only made worse by seeing the inquisitive stares of all three kids. *He was way out of his element here.*

"Eat your breakfast if you want to have time to play before your parents get here," he replied in his own defense.

Once the three went back to eating and talking amongst themselves, he went in search of the car seat. By the time Tommy showed up to get the girls a little before lunchtime, he felt like he had a better handle on the whole babysitting escapade. He could do this… anytime Carla needed him to. Besides with just the two boys it would be *much* easier.

Chuck had shown up within minutes of Tommy and the two stood talking until Tommy finally left with both girls. Greg then sent the boys up to pick up their rooms after mentioning their mother was less likely to allow Gretchen to stay overnight again, or any friend for that matter, if she was left with a mess to clean up. Once the boys could be heard upstairs in Matt's room, he began cleaning up the kitchen.

"I think working leather with Dickie's doing that arm some good," Chuck observed, pointing at Greg's injured shoulder.

He flexed his fingers and they somehow didn't seem as stiff as they normally did, though it was painfully obvious that for whatever reason the arm and hand would never be what they once were.

That was fine. If Carla was brave enough to go to college then he too could find something else to do with his life. Working at the shop, even only part time, was therapeutic and he found himself really enjoying it. Dickie had taken to showing him how he designed and made custom seats for the bikes they built. Shockingly, Greg found he was actually pretty good at it. Perhaps not as good as Dickie, but with time, who knew?

"Yea, it's feeling pretty good today," he agreed. "How are the wedding plans coming?"

"We picked a cake and stuff so I think everything is all set now. Meredith called Dickie this morning and asked him to walk her down the aisle. So now *I* get to ask her grandpa if he'll perform the ceremony. I know we're all straight now but ole' Judge Patterson still makes me nervous as hell," Chuck laughed.

Greg listened as Chuck called Nathan Patterson and ask if he would perform the wedding ceremony for the man's only granddaughter. Chuck visibly relaxed after listening to Nathan's response. Would he ever be talking to Judge Patterson himself? Asking permission to be with his daughter? Sitting down at the bar, his thoughts and feelings for Carla threatened to overwhelm him. Hanging up the phone, Chuck began cleaning up where he'd left off.

"You ok there, man?" Chuck finally asked him after glancing at him inquisitively several times.

"She's never going to see that I'm worth it… that I can be there for her because she doesn't need me to be there for her. I can barely be trusted with four children for a couple of hours, while she could probably handle a hundred kids all at the same time. My retirement and savings is nowhere near the kind of money her first husband made. She's family oriented and I'm a recovering workaholic," he gushed. "She's used to a man who can take care of her… I can barely take care of myself."

"Dude… you are going about this all wrong," Chuck replied.

"What do you mean?" he asked.

"You are better at getting her to loosen up and just… *live* a little bit… than anyone I know. Hell if not for you she would *never* have taken a real ride on my bike. She still acts like she didn't like it but I know she did. She lights up better than the Christmas tree in there, which I still haven't taken down, whenever you're around. I think she's just afraid to care about you for fear of losing you too. I completely get that… been there… done that. The thing is, she and Meredith made me realize that if I wanted a family I had to share things about myself and have a little trust that everything would work out. Now I talk to them about how I feel and they seem to really like that shit. You should try it… tell Carla how much you want to get with her and don't back down or let her talk you out of it because she's good at that," Chuck explained. "I'll bet you a fifty you could talk her into using that tattoo gift certificate I gave her for Christmas if you really tried… she likes it when you dare her to really *live*."

How long he sat there lost in thought, he wasn't sure but at some point he realized of all the advice the guys had given him about Carla... Chuck's advice was the most on target. The best times he'd had with Carla were when he was trying to get her to put aside her prim and proper behavior and just go for it. Be it school or *sex*... daring Carla was not only enjoyable but drew her to him.

He had dared her to go to school and that had resulted in an excited ball of fun that she was enjoying even now... he knew that. He just needed to prove his worth by helping her with the boys now that she'd taken his dare. *Would that work in other areas too?*

Carla followed Edna into the hospital room and almost laughed out loud. Bobby Jackson sat in a chair near the window holding a tiny infant in his large hands as though he was offering the child up to the heavens. He was talking softly to the baby in an obvious attempt to keep it from crying and waking Lilly who slept in the hospital bed nearby.

"Do you see this shit? Dana leaves me alone with him for ten minutes to go get some breakfast and he knows it and wants to act up," Bobby said quietly to Edna.

The older woman made her way over to the man who easily made two of her and said, "Most times babies cry because they are hungry, have a dirty diaper, are tired, bored or were startled by something. You're a daddy now so which one is it? It's not like you haven't done this already with Gretchen."

Bobby looked thoughtful for a moment and then, as though comforted by the fact that Edna wouldn't allow him to completely mess up, carefully readjusted the tiny infant up against his massive chest. He began patting the baby who instantly settled down. Looking at Edna he gave a half grin.

"It'll come back… you got off easy with Melody because Tommy's got Ms. Dana now but this one here is yours and you'll do just as good for him as you did for Gretchen," Edna said matter of fact and then shuffled over to where Lilly lay to press her frail hand against Lilly's forehead.

Carla walked over and blocked Edna and Lilly from Bobby's view when she heard the older woman ask Lilly a personal question. Leaning down she said, "He's absolutely perfect. How much does he weigh?"

Though she already knew most of the details from Chuck she listened to Bobby's description of his son and continued asking questions while Edna helped Lilly to the restroom. The old woman was like a childhood blanket, always warm, comforting, and full of wisdom. Once the bathroom door closed behind Lilly and Edna, Carla said, "Why don't you let me sit with him for a minute and you go get something to eat or a coffee or maybe a gift from the gift shop?"

Taking the hint, Bobby allowed her to take the tiny infant from him and then was gone in the next second. She sat holding the baby until Lilly finished up and she and Gran exited the bathroom. Lilly looked a little pale but still very beautiful for having just given birth.

She asked Gran about ten questions in quick succession as though she'd been waiting for the old woman to show up... or Bobby to leave. Gran answered each one the best she could and Lilly's relief that all was as it should be was written on her face as she lay back down in the hospital bed.

"I just don't think he's getting anything or I'm just not doing it right," Lilly finished, relaxing back against the pillow on the bed.

"Ms. Carla, why don't you bring that little guy over here and let's see if between the three of us if we can get him to eat a little better," Edna suggested.

After several attempts and encouragement from Edna, the baby was able to successfully nurse. Even more of Lilly's anxiety disappeared and was eventually replaced with a smile. Edna had yet to hold her grandbaby but that's not what she'd come for... she was playing surrogate mother to Lilly. She was giving advice and encouragement that a mother would give to her daughter at such a time. If it was possible to respect the old woman anymore, Carla did in that moment.

By the time Bobby and Dana returned, Edna had answered all of Lilly's questions, helped Lilly successfully feed her son, changed the baby, and had it swaddled and back in the bassinet. Edna looked a little tired from all the activity but smiled the smile of an angel. Bobby set some flowers down on a stand near Lilly's bed and bent down and kissed her forehead.

"How were the girls for you last night?" Dana asked Carla.

"They were perfect. The baby even slept through the night even though it was a strange environment for her," she replied.

"Well we owe you so if you ever need anything, just ask," Dana smiled.

"Actually... I was curious if you would be willing to help Ben with some of his schoolwork. He has a hard time staying on task at school and talks too much so his grades aren't what they should be," she said.

"Sure, anytime! I'm home all day so just let me know when is a good time for you and then just bring him on by," Dana replied. "Tommy said Gretchen really had a good time with your boys so maybe sometime soon they can stay over at our house."

"How about next weekend?" she asked. "I have a copy of the to-do list that Meredith gave me for Chuck's event and I haven't done *any* of my items yet."

"You know we could do a trade-off. Your boys could stay overnight at our house one weekend night a month and perhaps Gretchen could stay with you one weekend night a month in return," Dana suggested.

"That's a great idea, but it's only fair if I keep both the girls since you'd have both of my boys. Besides, it would give you a little bit of alone time with Tommy," she replied.

"Okay... but if that ends up being too much don't be afraid to say something," Dana said.

"They'll be fine. I haven't had a little girl around since Meredith was little. It'll be fun!" she replied.

They visited for a little while and then Carla took Edna out for lunch before taking her back home. After making sure that Edna was settled in she hurried home. Poor Greg had been with the boys quite a bit over the past twenty four hours. Her cell phone rang and, pulling over into the parking lot of a gas station, she answered upon seeing her father's name on the display.

"Hey, Daddy! Sorry I didn't get back to you... things have been crazy!" she explained.

"No big deal. I just wanted to tell you before you happened to see it on the television or in the paper that Jarrod Tompkins has spilled the beans about Doug and me paying him to be on his way all those years ago. There will be those who will say that being a judge I should have turned him in, even though I wasn't a judge back then, so I just wanted you to be prepared for it. Mudslinging is never fun... but even though I choose not to participate doesn't mean the opposing political party won't go after me with all they have."

What could she say? One bad choice twenty five years ago was still hanging over her head like a big dark rain cloud. It had rained on Chuck's showcase in New York and now it was raining on her father's career. She couldn't go back and undo the damage. She would just have to face it. Greg was right... if she dealt with it now it might finally be over for good.

"I'm so sorry, Daddy," she said.

"Stop apologizing for another person's stupidity, Carla. I chose to do what I did back then. We all make mistakes... even judges. Either the general public will accept that along with my apology for not having dealt with him back then or they won't. If not, I may just need to step up my retirement plans a little bit. That's all," her father replied.

After hanging up with her father she found herself driving home a little slower than before. Her thoughts were scattered and her heart breaking that a profession her father both loved and was good at might possibly be ruined because of Jarrod Tompkins. It wasn't right to hate... but people like Jarrod made that concept even harder. Her father would now be forced to make public appearances, which he hated, in an effort to salvage his reputation... which also meant he wouldn't be available to help her with the boys as much. *What else?* She felt tears gather but swallowed them back down.

Pulling into the driveway, again she found the boys in the side yard passing the football back and forth while Greg sat on the porch with a glass of tea coaching them. She made her way to the chair next to Greg's and sat down. He smiled in triumph at obviously having held down the fort just fine while she'd been at the hospital with Edna.

"How's the baby and Lilly?" he asked.

"They're both doing great... healthy and happy. How were the boys? Did they behave themselves for you?" she asked in return.

"Perfect angels," he grinned and then picked up a piece of paper from the side table between the two chairs and handed it to her. "Meet Ben's new coach."

"What?" she asked, taking the paper and scanning it briefly. It was a notification that two additional coaches were needed for the football league as soon as possible.

"This is a pretty big commitment and for at least six weeks…" she started.

"I called Dickie and he's in as well. I figure I'll call tomorrow and find out what's required to sign us both up," Greg interrupted. "I mean, what else am I going to do with my time now that I'm retired? I'm only forty five!"

"If you're trying to impress me… you don't need to do *this*," she argued, waving the paper at him.

Frowning at her, he said, "I'm doing this because Chuck and Meredith don't have the time right now and besides… Ben asked *me*… not *them*."

"I figured you would stay in New York after the premiere… how long are you planning on staying down here?" she asked. Six weeks was a long time to be pelted with his good looks on a regular basis.

"I'm renting the beach house from Becca for a while. With her down here now and me retired… there's not much to keep me in New York," he smiled. *God that smile.* "Matt's going to be my assistant so I figure since I'll have them both three nights a week for practice… it effectively takes care of your sitter needs. How's that for impressing you?"

For someone who had never wanted kids to sign up to be a football coach for six and seven year old boys was not only surprising but probably not a good idea. Even Doug had never volunteered for those types of things, mostly because with his job there hadn't been time, but also because he had known his limitations.

Greg had no idea what he was in for. He would figure that out much like he had while caring for baby Melody.

By the following Thursday evening before she left for class, Greg and Dickie were both signed up and would be working with Ben's team. Carla felt a little better knowing at least there would be the two of them to deal with all those little boys on the team, rather than just Greg having to adjust on his own. After class she hurried home to find Greg and the boys eating grilled hamburgers and corn on the cob at the table while discussing the first football practice. She was a little surprised that not only had he made it through meeting all the boys on the team but had managed to make dinner as well.

"Dana called and asked if the boys would be staying with them this weekend. I told her I'd have you call her when you got home," he said after she made herself a plate and sat down at the table with them.

Carla had expected there to be all sorts of issues with dinnertime, homework, showers or getting to bed on time but the boys seemed to adjust well to her being gone for class... even with football practice. Though things were done differently than before she started school, the boys had adjusted in relatively little time and didn't seem to be put out, at least not as much as she had anticipated.

She had just started to think that Greg was a natural family man regardless of his comment about not wanting kids, when cleaning up after dinner she found a hand written note from Chuck in the trash that included a suggestion for grilling hamburgers for dinner.

After calling Dana back and setting up a time to drop the boys off the following evening, Carla went upstairs to tuck the boys in for the night. She decided it was high time to ask what they really thought of Greg, since the two of them had been spending a large amount of time with him recently. Entering Matt's room first, she was surprised to find him holding a small video camera and watching the screen intently.

"Where did you get that, Matt?" she asked.

"Greg got it for me to use to record the practices with so we can study the plays and see how to help the team get better," he explained.

"You should have given it back to him before he left," she said.

"No, he said I should hang on to it and learn how to use it real good so I could make movies with it," he replied. "Don't worry I'll be really careful with it."

Hearing the excitement in her middle son's voice made her feel a little guilty. Between Meredith's injuries after the accident and Ben being the youngest, Matt often got squeezed out. It wasn't that Carla cared any more for the other kids or any less for Matt but he was less needy than the other two. If not for Chuck and now Greg it would seem it was quite possible for Matt to simply get lost in the craziness of their lives.

"Did you have fun at Ben's practice this afternoon," she coaxed.

"Yea, I showed Greg some videos on the computer of other little kids playing football yesterday and he said recording the practices and games would be a good idea. So after school today we went to the store and he told me to pick a camera because he doesn't know anything about them, so I picked this one and I taped the first practice already. I helped Ben with his homework while Greg was making dinner so I didn't get a chance to copy it on to the computer so he told me to just hang on to it since I'm better at operating it anyways," Matt explained.

Sitting down on Matt's bed, she watched the video on the tiny screen over his shoulder and was amazed at how clear it was and how well Matt had captured the events of practice. While Ben might have a natural talent at football, obviously Matt's gifts lay in the realm of technology. He voluntarily put the camera away after they watched most of the video.

"Looks like Greg handled all the kids pretty well," she again coaxed.

"They like him... Ben and I do too. He's fun and smart about boy stuff," Matt supplied.

After tucking Matt in and turning off his light she headed down the hall to Ben's room and found her youngest fast asleep. Bending down, she kissed his little cheek and pulled the blanket out from around him in order to tuck him in more comfortably.

Clutched in his little hands was the hard football that Greg had bought for him to replace the softer one they had been using. The image brought home the idea that the boys needed a male figure in their lives.

While her father had been a huge help with the boys since Doug's death, he wasn't around them all the time. Chuck, though equally helpful, was more like an older brother to them than any type of parental figure. Greg recognized each of her boys' strengths and weaknesses and tried to encourage the strengths and help them cope with the weaknesses… *like a parent.*

Turning off Ben's light, she headed back downstairs and stopped in the kitchen upon finding the crinkled up piece of paper that Chuck had written instructions on for Greg laying on the table. It was turned over and a handwritten note on the backside caught her eye. Picking up the note she read it to herself.

Not all of us have twenty years of experience at running a household but working as a team, I think we are doing just fine… so stop worrying. – Greg. PS… If you're free tomorrow night, how about that dinner that was part of your Christmas gift? The beach house at seven… see you then.

She couldn't help but smile. While she had twenty years of experience at running a household... he had twenty years of experience at asking women out... and he was good at it.

With the boys staying overnight with Gretchen... Carla would be alone with Greg for the first time since their night in New York. Her stomach was literally doing flips at the memory of being in his arms.

The following evening when she arrived at the beach house for dinner, Greg invited her inside, handed her a glass of wine and directed her back outside to a small, private alcove along the beach.

The little secluded area had a fallen log that looked as though it had been strategically placed there just so a person could sit on it and enjoy the sights, sounds and smells of the ocean. It was beautiful and breathtaking. She got lost in the serenity of the area and didn't hear Greg approach until he stood right next to her.

"Such a beautiful day... warm for this time of year... this is just incredible," she breathed, closing her eyes in enjoyment.

"Lean back against the branch," he said.

She glanced back behind her and seeing a good sized branch angling upwards off of the fallen log she did as he suggested. Before she knew what he was about he pulled the silk scarf from around her neck and tied it around her wrists. Bringing her hands up above her head he tied the ends together around a smaller branch that stuck off the main branch. Then as her heartbeat picked up speed he dropped to his knees in the sand in front of her and slid his hands up the outsides of her legs, bunching her sundress up around her waist.

As his hands found the sides of her panties and began to work them off with twenty years of experience she heard herself say, "Greg… what are you doing?"

Using his good arm he tilted her hips closer to the edge of the log and slid her panties all the way off at the same time. Then leaning forward so that his perfect lips were right against her cleft he said, "Changing your mind about being retained by a cop. And ensuring you don't use those talented hands of yours against me."

All protests escaped her mind when that *mouth* closed around the nub at the very center of her. Creating an electrical shock that went straight down the insides of both thighs to pool at the back of her knees.

Gasping in both shock and pleasure at the feel of him there, she was forced to use her hands to hold on to the each side of the smaller branch she was tied to in order to keep from falling off. Her legs began to shake at the exquisite bliss building in the very core of her.

With both hands now effectively holding on to a branch over her head while her back arched against the base of the branch, she could not stop looking down at him. Her legs were being held open wide by a sun kissed man with hazel eyes.

She both watched and felt the pleasurable heat that his mouth was creating in her until absolute ecstasy spiraled out in an explosion. As the intensity of the best orgasm she'd experienced in a long time began to fade he gently bit her bare thigh and whispered, "Dinner is ready."

Dinner? Not now!

After untying her and helping her up from the log he draped her scarf across one broad shoulder and stuffed her panties into the pocket of his jeans. He led her back up to the house by one of the hands he'd tied to the branch. After closing the door that led to the beach behind them she noticed the dinner table was already set.

Her body was on fire for him and he expected her to eat dinner as though two minutes earlier her body hadn't been skyrocketing towards heaven?

Turning toward him she wrapped an arm around his neck and kissed him with everything she had while guiding one of his hands under her shirt. She needed more of him... more of his hands on her in the worst possible way. Having enjoyed him in New York she had obviously missed being with him like this more than she was willing to admit... at least until now.

His breathing changed as she continued to kiss him. Begging him silently for what she needed as she helped him undress her and then himself. They managed to make it to the cold marble floor amidst a scattered pile of clothing. Just as he was about to claim her like she wanted him to, he stopped.

"I love you, Carla," he gasped out between her kisses while brushing her hair back from her face. "Say it back... *say* it to me, Carla. Tell me I'm not the only one who feels this thing between us."

"I know you do and I'm sorry I couldn't say it before but you know that I love you too. You have to know that... *feel* that. I didn't think I *could* love again but I can't help it anymore," she whimpered into his mouth.

Saying the words out loud was like opening up not only her body to his invasion but her heart as well. As he nudged between her legs trapping her against the hard floor and pushed himself within her, she heard herself say, "I do, Greg... I love you too."

Freeing her heart and mind to the idea of both being loved by another man and loving him in return unleashed a torrent of emotions in her that had her clutching at his back and pulling his bottom to her as he moved within her.

Again she broke apart crying out her love for him again and again until his own release had him doing the same. It felt like a mating of souls as she held him to her. *God she did love this man!* She didn't want to know the end before the beginning anymore. She was finally ready for a new journey.

Chapter Thirteen

"Why do I let her talk me into this shit?" Chuck asked Greg while staring at himself in the full length mirror that was attached to the door of the guest bathroom in the beach house.

Unsure what to say to the young man who wore loose fitting khaki swim trunks, a white shirt and tan sandals, Greg instead remained quiet. The young couple's need to mess with each other was way too funny but sexy all at the same time. From the look on Chuck's face, Meredith had won this round. Chuck actually looked really nice in a casual sort of way if not for the frown he wore. Greg decided against mentioning that fact.

"Could've been a suit or a tux and tails," he offered instead as an even worse alternative.

"Edith better be glad she's so cute and shit," Chuck continued. "She's got me on just as short a leash as Carla has you on, my man, so I guess we better get this show on the road."

The door opened and Ben and Matt came in to the room wearing nearly identical outfits to the one Chuck wore. Seeing the frown on Matt's face, Chuck said, "This was your *sister's* idea so if you've got an issue with looking like cabana boys go take it up with her."

"We're not allowed in there," Matt supplied.

"Yea… but I could get in there if I *wanted* to. Gretchen isn't strong enough to keep me out. Is she, Matt?" Ben asked, appearing irritated at what Greg could only guess was yet another disagreement between the pack of kids.

"Just ignore her, Ben. If you let her know that what she does and says makes you mad, she'll just keep doing it," Matt advised.

After a few last minute checks that everybody was ready they all headed downstairs and out the back door toward the beach. Seeing Tommy and Bobby dressed much the same as Chuck and the boys plus wearing equally grim expressions made Greg smile. Bobby passed off the infant in his arms to Sherri Simons after she handed Greg a packet of tissues. Sherri then went and found a seat. Tommy handed Melody off to Becca and then joined them as well.

"Enjoy it while you can, buddy… soon enough Carla will have you doing shit you would never dreamed of too… mark my words," Bobby said to Greg. "Though I doubt anyone is quite as whipped as *Charlie* here."

Though they didn't know it, Carla already had Greg eating out of her hand. Since the weekend they'd spent in this very house, when she had finally said the three words he had wanted to hear so badly, everything between them had changed. Most of the changes were for the better.

The only part that hadn't changed was that while all the other guys in this group were in committed relationships with the woman they loved, he was reduced to scheduling time with Carla. Each time he tried to bring up the subject of taking their relationship to the next level... be that moving in together or even *marriage*... she always said the same thing.

"It's just not a good time right now."

Greg could only hope that once this wedding was over maybe it *would be* a better time and he could get what *his* heart desired most... *Carla by his side.*

"Hey, man, this was the better of the two outfits she picked out!" Chuck said in his own defense to the other guys.

"You need to grow a set, man... Bobby's right... she's got you by the short hairs," Tommy laughed at Chuck just before Gretchen made it to the sand and reached Chuck's side.

The little girl was cute wearing a one piece swimsuit with a tiny floral wrap around her waist that acted as a skirt of sorts and flip flops with a big flower on each one. Her hair was braided down the back and hung to one side of her neck with a flower matching the ones on her flip flops on the other side of her head just above her ear. Aside from the dirty looks she was giving Matt and Ben she was absolutely adorable.

The guys had made a wooden boardwalk aisle and platform of sorts that would make it easier for Meredith to get to the decorated canopy that had been set up on the beach to house the young couple during the ceremony. White wicker chairs had been placed on each side of the aisle. Matt would unroll a runner down the boardwalk and Ben would follow after with a large open clam shell that held a small pillow containing the rings.

After winning the staring contest with the boys, Gretchen finally looked away from the two of them and up at Chuck and said, "Are you ready to promise to love and obey Ms. Meredith now, my Chuckie?"

This brought forth howls of laughter from Tommy and Bobby. Attempting to ignore them, Chuck took Gretchen's hand and headed up the boardwalk with the tiny girl trailing behind him staring at the rows of people on either side until they stopped underneath the canopy.

The wedding was a small, private affair with only close friends and family. Greg knew most of the guests there except for people from Doug's family and a few of Meredith and Carla's friends.

The crowd quieted down when Tommy and Bobby followed Chuck under the canopy and then stood next to Gretchen. When all of the guests figured out that the little girl who stood holding the groom's hand was acting as his best man rather than a flower girl, a collective sigh of adoration was followed by whispering.

Greg paused to look at the image the guys made. Even in the completely uncharacteristic outfits they wore there was no mistaking either their masculinity or the deep friendship they all shared.

He made his way to the front row to sit next to Carla. Upon seeing the tears swimming in her eyes already, he pulled the small pack of tissues out of his pants pocket that Sherri Simons had given him and offered her one. She smiled at him and took his offering just as Lilly Jackson made it down to the sand.

She was dressed in similar fashion to Gretchen, though her wrap was decorated with a different kind of flowers. She looked amazing for having given birth only five weeks prior. She walked down the aisle and winked at Bobby before taking her place on the opposing side of where the guys stood.

Dana Atkinson was next. She was dressed the same with yet another type of flower on her wrap and she took her place next to Lilly. Next to join the group was a friend of Meredith's from college named Ashley that came by the house from time to time to hang out.

A disgruntled noise escaped both Tommy and Bobby followed by snickers from Lilly and Dana as Meredith finally exited the house on Dickie's arm. Unlike themselves, Dickie wore jeans and a button up shirt.

Their displeasure at having to wear the outfits Meredith had chosen when Dickie did not have to was quickly replaced with a smile upon seeing the glowing woman on the older man's arm. Meredith had talked often about an idea she had that by getting married on the beach her father's presence would be there.

If that was in anyway true, then Greg knew that Doug Johnson must be a proud man right about now. Meredith was beautiful and wore a smile that was only outdone by the sun that chose that moment to shine through the clouds.

Meredith looked up at the sun and then at Dickie and said something that caused the older man to put an arm around her shoulders. The bride to be rested her head on his shoulder briefly before the two of them started toward the beach.

From an outsider looking in, the whole scene might seem weird but to Greg he understood the whole story and was happy that Dickie could be there for the young woman on her special day.

Unafraid and glowing like the beacon from a lighthouse, Meredith stepped onto the boardwalk in a light crème colored sleeveless gown that looked like it might have been made from some type of crinkled linen fabric that hit her just below the knee.

It was unusual and stunning against her sun bronzed skin. Looking back quickly Greg watched as a grin broke out on Chuck's face when his gaze met Meredith's.

Love, happiness and forever were etched on the faces of the young couple and as Meredith made her way down the aisle Greg looked down at Carla standing next to him. On Carla's face shown pride and a bittersweet smile. So Greg gently placed his hand on her shoulder to support her as she watched her only daughter be given away. She glanced at him again with a question in her eyes.

Leaning down Greg said quietly against her hair, "I have no doubt he sees her... she was right."

With that Greg handed the soft hearted woman he loved another tissue. He no longer felt like he was competing with a dead man's memory but instead hoped to win the same affection from Carla that she'd held for her first husband.

The fact of the matter was for the first time he felt how much the man had lost that day in addition to his life. This was one of those irreplaceable moments but if he were in Doug Johnson's place, he'd be here. So there was no doubt in Greg's mind that the man was here, in spirit if not in body.

The ceremony went off without a hitch and neither the bride nor the groom promised to obey the other. This caused several snickers including one from Carla who at some point during the ceremony had slipped her small hand into his.

When Nathan Patterson proudly announced the newly wedded couple the cheers from the crowd were heartfelt, loud and followed by laughter at Gretchen who was dancing around in her excitement.

Tables had been set up underneath a single large awning further down the beach. After congratulating the happy couple the guests walked along the beach and found a table to sit at for the reception. It was a slightly informal affair but beautiful and definitely represented the couple well. As evening fell paper lantern globes were lit which added to the romantic feel of the night.

Chuck and Meredith were all smiles and laughter as they made their way from table to table visiting with guests and family. After sharing a dance together on a makeshift dance floor that the guys had also put together because sand was a little tricky for Meredith to maneuver around on, Chuck danced with Gretchen while Meredith showed off her dancing skills with Tommy. Soon enough, the entire wedding party was up dancing. It was hard not to be taken in by the happy couple until you forgot yourself and joined right in on the fun.

Greg was able to get Carla to dance with him after she introduced him to her former in-laws who smiled approvingly at him. While he had hoped to hear from Sergeant Miller before the couple left for their honeymoon, it wasn't looking like that was going to happen. Now that the money had been found and Jarrod had pled guilty to a lesser charge to avoid potentially doing even more time, Greg had hoped to get the funds released so he could present it to Chuck and Meredith as a wedding present.

Knowing that the majority of the funds were there would be a real relief to them both but knowing how the law worked Greg didn't want to open his mouth until he had the money in his hands.

Though Carla refused to ride with him, Greg rode his new custom motorcycle with the group when they left the beach house to take the newly wedded couple to the airport. Carla instead drove her car that was loaded up with the luggage along with Gretchen and the boys who insisted on coming along to watch the airplanes.

Tommy had taught Dana to ride and she would be bringing Tommy's bike back from the airport while he rode Chuck's bike. Sherri had offered to keep both Melody and the newest addition to the clan while they were gone.

By the time the airplane actually taxied out for takeoff all three kids had to be woken up to watch. This resulted in Gretchen having to be carried out of the airport by her dad after insisting she was too tired to walk. Ben was also looking like he was about to fall over but Greg knew his shoulder couldn't handle the stout little guy.

Saving him from having to admit that fact or even say anything, Bobby stepped up instead and hefted Ben over his shoulder. Matt had insisted on walking and by the time the group made it back to the beach house Greg insisted that the boys and Carla stay there with him for the night.

The boys were asleep in the spare room before the last car pulled out of the driveway. It had been a great day and he knew that Carla was tired so he offered her one of his t-shirts and she was also asleep within minutes.

He lay awake for a few moments enjoying the feeling of her leg draped over his and her slender arm across his chest. To have this every night was just a dream up to this point because it had never been the right time. *Would it be the right time now?*

When he awoke to the feel of her in his arms, it was even better than having fallen asleep with her. She had felt good in his arms even back in New York the first time she'd spent the night with him. This third time had him realizing that he couldn't let her leave again with shoes in hand.

"Are you awake, beautiful?" he asked quietly.

"Yes… I was just lying here enjoying you before I get the boys up for breakfast," she whispered against his chest. "You feel amazing… so warm."

"You could have this every morning… all you have to do is say the word," he replied. "Marry me, Carla. Give me a chance to make you happy."

Sighing heavily she said, "If only it were that easy."

"Why isn't it that easy?" he asked.

Looking up at him she said, "Becca didn't tell you?"

"Tell me what?" he replied.

"Chuck used the money from the sale of his first two paintings to pay off the mortgage on the house. I can't just move them out and you in. The original lease on his apartment is up now and the landlord wants him out. Even Becca's continued threats to take that judgmental bastard to court can't buy Chuck more time now that the lease is up. I feel like I need to let them stay at the house as long as they want or need to after they spent every dime they had to help me out. Do you understand that?" she said. "It has nothing to do with not loving you and not wanting to be with you but I feel like I should either give them the house and find a place of my own first or… something."

"Is that why you keep turning me down?" he asked in disbelief.

"That and…" she said and then quit talking and instead snuggled up closer to him.

"Tell me, Carla. Whatever it is I'll do what I have to in order to be with you," he persuaded.

"I know you're not in law enforcement anymore but you've simply replaced one danger with another one and I can't bear to lose another husband… I just can't," she explained in a rush.

"Hey… hey… what makes you think I'm in any danger?" he asked.

"Your motorcycle! You ride it really well, I can see that… but other drivers…" she said. "I saw that guy pull out in front of Bobby yesterday and I… if something happened to you," she finished in a whisper.

"Life is one big game of chance, Carla. *There are no guarantees.* The only thing I can promise you is that as long as I'm on this earth and you want me… my heart is yours. How long I've got on this earth isn't up to me. I have to believe that because there is no other explanation on why instead of killing me that bullet only messed up my shoulder and forced me out of a job. I should have died that night… you heard the doctor before they took me back to surgery," he said. "That motorcycle… those guys at the shop… they have given me another option besides carrying a gun and a badge. I like working at the shop and I love my bike. If you love me then you have to love my hopes, dreams and goals too… even if they change from time to time. I love you because you're a middle aged mother of three… *four*… going to college for the first time."

Even though Carla didn't reply her heart was listening… he could *feel* it. He only hoped that for once instead of busting his balls in court, his sister's chosen profession would *benefit* him.

Becca had more money than she knew what to do with. Yet instead of living in this amazing beach house, she was content to live in a little plat house that was smaller than the living room of her old apartment in New York. That concept amazed him more than her offer to sell him the beach house for what she still owed on it.

"Becca offered to sell me this place. In fact she offered me an amazing deal on it. I'm thinking about taking her up on it. I realize it's only two bedrooms and not nearly big enough for two growing boys but do you think it might be big enough for Chuck and Meredith?" he asked.

"What are you saying?" she asked after rolling off of him and then poking him in the ribs.

"I'm saying if I bought this place for them, wouldn't that make you guys even? A house for a house?" he laughed. "How cool would it be to look out your back door and see not only the ocean but the very beach you were married on?"

A beautiful smile lit up her eyes which then dropped to his mouth when he returned the gesture. He would never ever grow tired of her staring at his mouth as long as he lived. Rolling over on top of her, he then wedged himself between her shapely legs. Reaching down he pulled the t-shirt she'd worn to bed up so that he could taste one of her beautiful breasts. When he had her writhing beneath him, he pulled back from her.

"Is that a yes, Carla?" he asked before sucking a pebbled nipple back into his mouth.

"Greg… please…" she whispered.

"Answer me. If I take Becca up on her offer for this house and then give it to Meredith and Chuck, will you take *me* in then?" he whispered after releasing her breast again. "I'll essentially be homeless if I do that."

"Yes… yes I will take you in if you do that for them… now please don't make me beg you for it," she whispered against his good shoulder while trying to position his hips where she wanted him most.

Her squirming body beneath his own forced him to grit his teeth in order to keep from caving in and taking her. *A firecracker was what she was.* She wasn't going to do that to him this time. Not until he had his say and got some answers from her… got a commitment in return.

"How do I know you won't just kick me to the curb? I could end up paying rent on a park bench or for the basement apartment under a pier at the beach," he teased. "If you married me... then I'd feel *safer*. How about it, Carla? I *dare* you… *marry* me."

"I'll marry you this afternoon if you will please just…" she whimpered against his neck while lifting her hips up toward him.

"Do you mean that?" he asked, forcing her to be still by putting more of his weight on her.

Raising her head up she looked first at his mouth and then into his eyes before kissing him. When she finished with him and laid her head back against the pillow she said, "You forget my father is a judge in this town and can perform marriages… so yes I mean it."

"No big wedding… with all the fancy stuff women usually want?" he asked.

"The only thing I want right now is you between my legs," she said. "If you want all that stuff since you've never been married before that's fine but it'll take longer."

"God, Carla... hearing that kind of stuff coming out of your mouth makes me crazy," he said, leaning his forehead against one slender shoulder.

"Oh yea? Prove it, Detective," she whispered into his hair.

Moving forward he slid his good arm under her body and around her waist and lifted her bottom up to better position her to take him. Then in one steady move he pushed into her. Feeling how ready her body was for him had him nearly losing it.

Instead he again forced her to be still beneath him. Over and over again he brought her to orgasm while refusing to follow until he just couldn't do it anymore... until there was no turning back. She was his... *finally*.

When the euphoria that was wrapped around his brain so tightly that it was making him dizzy began to fade, he could hear the television on downstairs. Carla must have heard it too at the same time. Instead of the reaction he expected out of her, which was to run out on him, she giggled softly against his arm.

"We're guests in your house this time... I'd like eggs and toast and some coffee," she said around her smile before kissing his arm.

After a quick shower he left her still lying there in his bed running her torturous hands down a body he wanted to taste yet again but couldn't. Instead he headed downstairs to make her breakfast and coffee. God, he *was* whipped even *worse* than Chuck ever thought about being. *The guys didn't need to know that though.* Then deciding to grow a set as Tommy had so delicately put it, he fished out his cell phone. While getting the coffee started he called Edna Jackson to get Nathan Patterson's phone number and then immediately dialed it after hanging up.

When the judge answered his phone and Greg informed him who he was the old man said, "I was wondering when I'd be hearing from you. You didn't waste any time did you?"

"No, Sir, she said yes and I'd like to take her up on that today if that's possible. Just in case she changes her mind and decides to string me along a little longer instead," he finished breathlessly.

"I'm going to have to make you wait for a couple more weeks myself then, Detective. For two reasons… one because Meredith will never forgive me if she isn't here to witness it and second because having your anniversary the day after your stepdaughter's anniversary is just weird, for lack of a better term," Judge Patterson laughed. "Besides, I have a golf outing this afternoon. I'm doing all I can to fix my reputation since, unlike myself, a certain ruthless detective couldn't let a criminal just walk away. Two weeks from today and she's all yours. You also might want to go downtown and get a marriage license."

"Yes, Sir, and thank you," he replied and disconnected the call.

"I take it Daddy said yes?" Carla said, wrapping her arms around his waist from behind.

"Yea… in two weeks!" he muttered with disappointment thick in his voice.

"Good… that'll give you time to ask the boys' permission," she said against his back.

"You're going to make me work for this aren't you?" he smiled, glancing back at her.

"Uh huh, now where's that coffee?" she smiled.

The two weeks waiting for Chuck and Meredith to get back from their honeymoon in Florence was the longest two weeks of Greg's entire life. Then knowing how anxious he was to get things moving along, Carla had insisted that he not say anything until after they'd had a chance to tell them all about their honeymoon. She was damn good at driving him crazy both in and outside of the bedroom.

Gretchen had begged to stay overnight with them so she could see her beloved Chuck. It felt like a year had passed while he, the boys and Gretchen waited for them to get back from the airport. Matt was happy to videotape Greg trying to make dinner while Ben ran head first into the oversized couch in the living room over and over again. Gretchen kept trying unsuccessfully to get Ben to stop it which seemed to have just the opposite effect.

Just as Greg thought he couldn't wait another minute for them to get home, especially once dinner was finished, he heard Ben yell, "They're here!"

Even Matt left him to go and record the newlyweds coming in the door instead. Forcing the eagerness Greg felt back down into the pit of his stomach and continuing to set the table while the happy couple and Carla made their way into the house was a lesson in self-control. Would Chuck and Meredith be happy for them? Would they accept him into their family? *Everyone knew about it but them.* Carla was obviously growing a little nervous at their reaction too based on the look she gave him upon entering the kitchen to help him finish up dinner.

The noise from the front of the house had grown to a nearly deafening level when he suddenly heard Gretchen say excitedly, "Mr. Sanders and Ms. Carla are in *love*, my Chuckie. I heard Mama and Aunt Becca talking about it. I wasn't listening in... I just heard Mama talking instead of the television and that's what they said."

"You're being nosy, Gretchen!" Ben said angrily.

"Shut up Bennie! I wasn't talking to you!" Gretchen said angrily.

"Hey, both of you knock it off," Chuck said. "Gretchen, we already knew that but you *were* being nosy and I'm pretty sure both your mama, Ms. Becca *and* Ms. Lilly have talked to you about that. Now you go on in there and apologize to Mr. Sanders and Ms. Carla."

Greg and Carla stared at each other nervously until Gretchen appeared in the kitchen with Ben right behind her. Ben stood rigidly behind the little girl with his arms crossed over his body wearing a look that said he was clearly in the right while Gretchen was very, *very* wrong. Then he loudly said to Carla, "Gretchen has to apologize for telling Meredith and Chuck about Mr. Sanders wanting to marry you!"

Chapter Fourteen

"Is that true?" Meredith asked Carla.

"Why don't we sit down and have some dinner and talk about it," she replied.

"Oh, Mama! That's so great! I may owe Charlie a hundred large now but I don't care! I'm so happy for you!" Meredith squealed while hugging Carla tightly.

Glancing at Greg, Carla watched Chuck smack him on the back as a big grin spread across his face. "Congratulations, man! When's the big day?"

"Come on let's sit down and eat while we talk," Carla again interjected.

Two hours later a decision had been made to go ahead and move Chuck and Meredith into the beach house the following weekend. This would give Greg and Carla a week to settle in together before actually exchanging vows. The weekend after that would be used to finish preparations for the auction event the group had been planning and organizing. Then the last weekend of the month was the actual date for the dinner and raffle of the painting.

With the whole group pitching in, no one person had been saddled with preparing for the event. Carla was used to normally handling everything herself but with this group, things seemed to just fall into place on their own. Each person had offered to help or provide something and she had only agreed or provided another suggestion. It was a whole lot less stressful than most of the parties she'd hosted while she'd been married to Doug. This brought about another change she was starting to like… learning to let go of what she couldn't control.

"Well we have some exciting news too," Meredith said.

Carla's heart nearly stopped. Seeing the look she knew was on her face but was unable to take back had Meredith scrambling to explain.

"No, not that! We decided on a charity to donate any of the funds we are able to collect to. God, Mom! We just got married!" Meredith laughed. "We talked about what to do with some of the money from the premiere and we want to start a charity of our own."

"Oh, well that's a good idea," she replied.

"Well I think I may have something that will help with both the dinner auction at the end of the month as well as your charity ideas," Greg cut in.

Carla watched him pull out a packet of papers and hand them to Meredith. After reading them she looked at Greg and said, "You found the stolen money?"

When Greg smiled at Meredith in affirmation, Carla noticed Chuck's face go from confused to an almost disappointed look. Knowing Chuck was unlikely to say what was bothering him based on how he sat back in his seat and stared at the table, Carla moved over closer to him taking the chair that Gretchen had given up when she and the boys headed upstairs to play.

"What is it, son?" Carla asked.

A look crossed the young man's face she couldn't read for once. He glanced at her and then looked away and appeared to be struggling with his emotions for a moment. When he finally turned back to her, she just wanted to hug him.

"Say that again... I got Dickie, which is cool as shit but... I've never had a... *mom*," he said.

Instead, she hugged him around his neck and said, "You're a part of this family now. That makes you my son."

He let her hug him this time where before a hug always caused a tension in him that made her just release him. When she let finally let him go he smiled his normal mischievous grin and said, "I think your sappy shit is rubbing off on me... *Mom*."

"Language... Mister!" Gretchen yelled from the living room.

"Mind ya business... Rudy!" Chuck yelled back at the little girl. "Does that mean the auction is off then? I mean if we can give those people back their money..."

"Look, you do what you think is right. If it hadn't been for me and my skeleton laden closet none of this would have happened to begin with," Carla replied.

"May I make a suggestion?" Greg interjected.

"You're fixing to be part of this big ass, weird family too, so that means you get to give unwanted advice, stick your nose in where it doesn't belong and share opinions on a whim. So go for it!" Chuck laughed.

"Why don't you have the dinner auction and tell the guests the truth... tell them what happened and offer to refund their money if they want it but also tell them about your charity and let them decide for themselves. Get a refund or let it go to your charity... that takes the weight off you," Greg replied. "If they see you doing the right thing... they might be more likely to do the right thing in return. They still get dinner and the chance at one of your paintings."

"That's a great idea... I, uh... I got to go paint for a minute," Chuck replied and then without a word got up from the table and headed for the front door.

"Hey! Husband! Are you forgetting something?" Meredith yelled at his retreating back as she stood up from the table.

A moment later Chuck returned, leaned down and hefted Meredith over his shoulder then started for the door. Once the happy couple left for Chuck's apartment, Carla turned from the door to find Greg leaving a message on Chuck's cell phone telling him where the extra key was to the beach house if they wanted to take a look. Looking at him she saw a future for the first time since Doug's death... a good future... full of love and family. That hadn't died with Doug... it had simply changed... grown to include more people.

"I should run Gretchen home so they don't have to get the baby out this late," Greg offered.

"Can't I stay one more night? I could go to Ben's football game tomorrow and watch it with you, Ms. Carla, so you don't get bored," Gretchen offered sweetly.

With Ben and Matt standing behind the tiny girl giving her equally pleading looks it was hard to deny them anything.

"Call your Daddy and ask him," Carla replied, handing Gretchen the house phone. She watched the little girl call Tommy as though she'd done it a million times. Gretchen was exceptionally smart, very aware of the world around her and would likely do amazing things one day.

Ben's first game of the season was an eye opener for Carla. Her little boy wasn't just the biggest player on the team but the best. It was obvious that his skill far surpassed the other kids on his team or even the opposing team. He almost appeared bored… but not so much that he didn't want to play.

Carla could feel Greg watching her from time to time as she looked on in awe of both of her sons. Matt was on the sideline with his camera in hand catching every play while his brother was the one making them. Rather than sitting with Carla and keeping her from being bored, Gretchen was on the sidelines standing next to Dickie yelling everything the older man said to the team.

She had been so worried that Dickie and Greg wouldn't be able to handle a team of kids since neither of them had children of their own... but they were like an oddity to the kids which helped Carla relax. The team swarmed them and both men talked to the little boys like they were professional athletes... or at least on their way to the pros.

Each time a kid would mess up she would watch both men laugh and the kids responded to that much better than the opposing coach who looked frustrated at his team. Greg and Dickie were having as much fun as the boys... and Gretchen.

Moving Chuck and Meredith out was an experience Carla wouldn't forget anytime soon. The entire group had shown up except for Dana who had offered to watch the boys so that none of the kids would be under foot. They had packed Meredith's belongings into Bobby's truck, some of the available cars and even a few things into Dickie's tow truck by mid-morning.

Carla was amazed by this considering all the clowning around that went on. Several of the neighbors had even come out to see what all the commotion was about and she'd only smiled and waved at them.

She finally gave up on stopping Greg from helping and joining in on the antics with the other guys. It was obvious who was in charge though, as Lilly sat on the tailgate of Bobby's truck instructing them which vehicle to put stuff into while Meredith directed them on what things she was taking and what should stay.

Becca offered Chuck and Meredith the use of the furniture that was already at the beach house. This resulted in Chuck cornering Becca for a hug while thanking her for 'giving up her goodies to him.' Having been on the receiving end of Chuck's inappropriate teasing, Carla felt for Becca.

Once they were done getting Meredith's belongings and the few items that Chuck had at the house, they all loaded up and headed for Chuck's apartment to pack his things up before heading off to the beach house.

As a retribution for forcing their friend, who just happened to have a criminal record and tattoos, out of his apartment, the guys made it a point to block the landlord's truck in his parking spot by pulling in on either side and then sideways directly behind him. Then they decided to take a lunch break. By the time they came out with stuff to load from the apartment the man was livid and threatening to call the police.

"Not to worry… it's moving day and I'm ready to blow this roach motel," Chuck advised the landlord. Then noting the couple standing next to the landlord holding an application for his apartment, Chuck continued, "Be careful… some of those things are pretty big… hence why I'm out of here. You don't have kids do you?"

Carla couldn't help but snicker as the couple handed the application back to the landlord and started toward their car. Whether they were turned off by the idea of bugs or by having neighbors like Chuck, Carla wasn't sure, but either way it was funny.

After Dickie moved his tow truck far enough back to allow the landlord to back out of his parking space, the man took off like he was being chased by the hounds of hell. Soon enough they all loaded up and took off for the beach house. Carla had offered to stay behind and clean up.

"Might want to take some pictures of the place to show it's in just as good of shape as it was before he moved in," Greg suggested to her after they finished cleaning the empty apartment. "Something tells me Chuck may have to take that prick to small claims court to get his deposit money back. Pictures and receipts for the rent should help his case."

"Actually, Dana is the one who would have to take him to court since the apartment was in her name. Besides Chuck wouldn't take him to court anyway… even if he did have a case against him. He'll just walk away having done nothing more than give the man a hard time and his middle finger," she replied.

"I've met a lot of people in my life… in my line of work. They all look like a big pack of trouble but really they are as down to earth and fun as anyone I've ever met aside from my buddy Rusty, the guy that helped find all the money. They're good people," Greg said. She could only smile and nod her agreement.

The morning of her wedding day, Carla woke with a start at the phone ringing. Answering the one next to her bed she was surprised to see Tommy and Dana's number on the display.

"I'm so sorry to bother you today of all days…" Dana started.

"No… no… its fine… just a formality really," Carla insisted.

"I was wondering if you thought possibly your father would consider marrying Tommy and I today as well? Casey Lawrence just gave birth a few hours ago and since the baby is in another county… The case worker, Carmen, says it would really help our chances if we were married rather than just living together," Dana said in an excited rush. "We'll have a real wedding later on but if your dad could marry us and maybe even sign this paper Carmen gave us, I… we would be so grateful."

"I'll call him but I don't think he would have a problem with it," she replied.

A few hours later at precisely eleven thirty Carla stood side by side with Greg in her father's office while a couple of feet away Tommy and Dana also stood hand in hand. This wasn't the big extravagant wedding that Doug had given her but as she reached down and grasped Greg's hand it felt more like a partnership this time around.

Greg had been right when he said she should support his goals and dreams as well… he was definitely supportive of hers… and the boys. A partnership was a good start in any marriage and a killer smile that made her think of the amazing chemistry they shared was just a bonus.

"What are they about?" he whispered to her, referring to Tommy and Dana.

"Tommy's ex-girlfriend had her baby last evening and they stand a good chance of it being placed with them since the mother's incarcerated. They are just solidifying that possibility along with their commitment to each other," she replied. An odd expression crossed Greg's face when Tommy explained to Carla's father about the little girl listed on the document her father held.

"Virginia Mae McMurray... or at least we hope someday she'll be a McMurray," Tommy said smiling at Dana who smiled right back at him.

"Ginny?" Greg asked his face showing even more confusion before it turned to a look of frustration.

"Yea... how'd you know that?" Dana laughed.

"Oh God... Sherri Simons! She has yet again pulled a fast one on me," Greg replied in defeat.

"What are you talking about?" Carla asked.

Greg glanced at Judge Patterson and then said, "Sherri called me yesterday on my way home from the shop and asked me to stop by the bar. When I got there she asked me if it was illegal to pay someone to give up the rights to their child. I told her that it wasn't that easy unless the parent was giving the child up for adoption but that sometimes an adoptive couple would pay for the biological parent's 'expenses' and she..." he paused as though unable to accept how well Sherri had played him. "Then she thanked me and said she was going to borrow money from her rich ass sister to go see about getting a little Ginny. I thought she meant... liquor."

It was bad but a giggle escaped her before she could stop it. After these last few months of hell that Jarrod had put her through… put them all through, Carla finally saw a point to it all. She had wondered what the point of hiding the truth about Jarrod from Meredith for all those years was when Meredith had found out anyways.

If Carla hadn't kept it a secret then none of her skeletons would have fallen out of her closet at just the right time… in front of the right people… and Sherri Simons would never have known to even try something like that. Though Sherri hadn't been at the premiere in New York, this group of people didn't keep secrets and Carla's secrets had actually served a purpose after all.

The more she thought about it the more she couldn't contain her laughter. Glancing first at Chuck and Meredith who stood at the back of the room and then at Greg she knew the minute Greg's mind picked up on the humor of the situation and he grinned too. Soon enough they were all laughing.

"Perhaps we should move things along a little in case there is more to this adventure for the two of you today," Judge Patterson said to Tommy and Dana.

Her father simply smiled at her and out of the corner of Carla's eye she could swear she saw her mother smiling in the painting behind her father's chair. Looking in Greg's eyes when he promised to love her for the rest of his life, she believed him because to be apart from him after all he'd done for her and the kids was the worst thing she could imagine at this point. He was a friend, a lover and now a husband.

When they left her father's office, Carla wished Tommy and Dana good luck with getting the new baby and then she left with Greg. It was decided that with school and everything else it would be best to postpone their honeymoon until the summer when whomever watched the boys wouldn't have to contend with homework and football.

The next couple of weeks were spent getting everything finalized for the dinner auction. By the time the morning of the event rolled around there wasn't much left to do. Carla hated that Chuck was so nervous about telling the guests about what had happened to their money. Meredith mentioned that she'd helped him write a speech and that he practiced it in front of a mirror every day.

When the house phone rang she picked it up without looking.

"Hi, Carla... we've got a little situation here," Dana said.

"What's wrong and what can I do?" she offered.

"Chuck says he can't go tonight... that he can't do this. He's afraid that if those people figure out he's not the eccentric person those New York news articles made him out to be that they'll be mad," Dana said. "I tried to talk to him and he just says he can't do it."

"Where is he now?" she asked.

"Upstairs lying on Gretchen's bed talking about how he feels sick to his stomach," Dana replied with a sigh.

"I'm on my way," she replied.

After hanging up the phone she turned around to find Greg leaning against the bar grinning at her.

"Go…" he said. "I can handle the boys… it's not like I have to feed them baby food or change their diapers. Take them to your father's house… check. Got it. Now go!"

Twenty minutes later she was welcomed into Tommy and Dana's home to find a tiny little infant girl in the swing. This little girl looked… healthy… *normal*… compared to Melody who was lying on her stomach on the floor.

"Your husband has ruined her," Dana laughed pointing at Melody. "Aside from the fruit she refuses to eat any baby food at all and insists on having whatever we are having. Funny thing is she has gained a pound and a half. The pediatrician said to keep doing whatever it is we are doing so Greg is safe for now."

Carla laughed and said, "I'll let him know."

When Melody fussed Dana picked her up and handed her to Carla saying, "I swear I think all three of them can *smell* him or something. She wants Chuck."

Inspiration took that opportunity to strike and Carla said, "I know your parents were going to watch the two little ones this evening but why don't they just come to the dinner this evening and help out with them instead?"

Understanding lit in Dana's eyes as Carla turned and headed up the stairs with Melody in her arms. Pushing the door to Gretchen's room open, Carla could only grin at Gretchen who was carefully placing what looked like a wet washcloth on Chuck's forehead.

"Ms. Carla, my Chuckie's too sick to go tonight," Gretchen said shaking her head.

"Well that's too bad. See I messed up big time and invited your Grandma and Grandpa Atkinson to the dinner tonight so it looks like Melody and Ginny will be going along as well. Since you three are going, I'm not sure I can tell Ben and Matt that they *can't* go… that wouldn't be very fair. What in the world are we going to do with all you kids running around with all those people and their fancy clothes…" she gushed.

"I'll be singing with Daddy so you don't gots to worry about me," Gretchen supplied. "Ben and Matt will just have to find someone else to play with or sit still and just watch me."

"Well with your daddy singing with you, and your mama filling in for Chuck since he's sick… I will need to keep an eye on the boys so we're going to have to find some more help with your sisters," she replied to Gretchen.

Peeling the wet washcloth off his forehead and flinging it at Gretchen who punched him in the leg in return, Chuck said, "Fine! You guys are killing me here and potentially ruining a career that hasn't even really started yet but I'll go!"

"You're a big fat faker, Charlie!" Gretchen yelled at him. "I'm telling Ms. Meredith and you'll be grounded forever!"

"I don't know at what point you got the impression that Meredith is in charge at *my* house but it's me… I'm the boss there… not her!" Chuck said to Gretchen who only put her hands on her tiny hips as though she didn't believe him.

"Is that so?" Meredith asked from the doorway as Melody tried to dive out of Carla's arms in an attempt to get to Chuck. Gretchen gave Chuck a knowing look as though she had tried to warn him.

Sitting up, Chuck took the baby from Carla's arms and Melody squealed in glee at him and clapped her little hands together.

"Well since we're going to have more guests I guess I should let Bobby and Tommy know to set up at least one or two more tables... for all the kids... alright, *boss?*" Meredith asked, giving Chuck a teasing smile before continuing. "Careful or I'll sit *you* at that table too!"

"Well in that case, since I *am* the boss of my house, I am wearing jeans... not clothes better suited for a preacher," Chuck replied with a self-satisfied smile.

On the way back to the house, Carla called Greg and asked him not to take the boys to her father's house after all but to have them wash their hands and faces instead and put on church clothes. Then she called her father and asked him to put on a suit as well and meet them at the dinner.

Chuck had said in New York that this auction would be done his way and somewhere in all the planning they had all lost sight of what Chuck's way meant... even her. *Casual, loud and lots of fun... that was Chuck.*

When she made it to the house and was presented with rumpled looking little boys, who looked more like they did *after* the Sunday service rather than before, accompanied by the single most handsome husband on the planet, she could only smile. Soon enough they were on their way to the auction and a feeling of peace filled her. Things were working out for her little family just the way they were supposed to.

The crowd that had gathered in front of the banquet facility were dressed much like those people in New York. Chuck on the other hand was dressed in jeans and t-shirt and, unlike in New York where he had been out of his environment, here he was in his element. A wide smile displayed on his face as he greeted people and shook their hands. She watched as the large group of people collectively relaxed… just like she had once she got to know him.

"He'll be just fine," Greg said.

"I know… I find it just as hard to cut the apron strings with him as I do with Meredith," she said.

"I got something you can use those apron strings for…" Greg replied with a flirty grin as he opened the car door.

Dinner went off without a hitch and the guests took to Chuck like a moth to a flame. A local radio and television station had shown up and Matt stood off to the side with them watching and mimicking what they did with his little camera. By the time it was time to unveil the painting Chuck had calmed down considerably. The entire place had somehow turned into one big party and the lines of elegantly dressed guests blurred with those who'd come in jeans.

Standing, Chuck walked up front and said, "Many of you received a letter about tonight's event that talked about the man who sold tickets to you for this dinner. This whole thing started as a scam... but for me it has turned out to be something pretty cool. My wife, Meredith, hooked me up with this speech but now that I've met you all I don't think I need it. What that letter didn't tell you was that most of the money has since been found."

Carla felt Greg's hand on her back as she tried to send Chuck good vibes of encouragement.

"I'd like you to know that you are welcome to a full refund of the money you paid for those tickets and consider tonight's dinner on me... or rather my family. If you are willing to though, I'd like you to instead be a part of this charity thing that I've been thinking about starting," Chuck continued. "I was a foster kid just like that tiny little baby in the back. When your little and cute like her... foster families or adoptive parents aren't as hard to get. You get to be a teenager though and it's slim pickings. Then one day you're essentially tossed out into the wild with little to no survival skills. I'd like to change that for as many kids as I can. Give them a place to go when they get out of the system, train them for a job and for life... just like one crazy biker and one righteous old lady did for me. Dickie Long and Edna Jackson helped me change my life. Say 'Hi' guys."

Dickie waved his hand in the air for a brief moment and Edna Jackson smiled and waved at Chuck and several people laughed at the old woman's playfulness with the young and extremely talented artist.

"This is something I really want to do. I'm hoping you'll let me keep the money you spent on those tickets to help another foster kid, like I used to be, see the sunshine through the rain," Chuck said, pulling the piece of linen cloth of the painting he'd done.

A gasp went through the crowd. What the room full of people were looking at would go down in history for sure. Of that Carla had no doubt. The painting showed a ray of sunshine breaking through a black cloud that was dumping rain down on a collection of flowers sticking out of a small flowerbed. The flowers were of various colors, shapes and heights… and each one was shying away from the rain and leaning into the sun. Chuck's heartfelt admission had just significantly increased the value of the painting and perhaps every other one he ever did from this point forward. Philanthropy always added value both for the giver and the recipient.

"If you want a refund, please see Lilly Jackson at the table over there. If you'd like to purchase another ticket for the auction, you can see my wife, Meredith, at that table. The first love of my life and owner of my heart… Gretchen McMurray… will draw the winning ticket in about a half an hour so enjoy the food and drinks," Chuck finished.

Gretchen was hoisted into the air by Tommy and she waved at the crowd and smiled a dimpled grin full of sugar and spice. Just as Carla's father stood from where he'd been sitting next to Edna Jackson and headed over to see Meredith with his check book in hand, Carla noticed Edna looking really pale. It was time to talk to the older woman about a nagging suspicion Carla had entertained since Thanksgiving dinner.

"I should go see about Edna," she said to Greg.

"Do what you have to beautiful… in the words of Chuck… I got your back!" Greg said with a smile and a cute nod of his head. Leaning down she stole a quick kiss from him before heading over to Edna.

Sitting down in the seat her father had vacated, Carla said, "You doing okay there, Ms. Edna?"

"Oh… just old," Edna replied. "Been having some problems today."

"Anything I can do for you," she asked.

"Maybe catch me a ride home with your father. He usually leaves these things pretty early too," Edna said.

"Sure… I'll take care of that. I don't know if Lilly mentioned it to you but I'm in school… for nursing… so if I can help… just ask. For all that you do for others… I really wouldn't mind at all," she offered.

Edna smiled at her with tears of gratitude shining in her eyes and said, "I suppose you've been around long enough to spot when a person's time is getting shorter, huh?"

Swallowing the lump in her throat, Carla simply nodded her head. Her suspicions had been right. Edna Jackson wouldn't be around forever and she had just confirmed it.

"Don't mention it to any of them… My life is a good one and I don't want that to change any sooner than it has too. If you can help with that… it's all I would need," Edna explained.

"It will stay between us. I'll stop by in the middle of the week and see how you are and we'll figure out a care plan for you and I'll see it done, when the time comes," she said.

Edna patted her hand before Carla stood to go and find her father to see about getting Edna home. Once her father and Edna left she settled back down in her seat next to Greg who smiled his sexy smile at her.

"What?" she asked.

"Do you have any idea how turned on I am right now?" he asked.

"From what?" she asked again.

"Watching you be all sweet and helpful to anyone and everyone all day today... knowing that when I get you alone tonight you'll turn into this tiger with an appetite that's... *amazing*. I never expected that from you and it's just one more thing I absolutely adore about you," he whispered with that mouth just a breath away from hers.

"Falling in love with you was totally unexpected for me too... so I guess that makes us even... *Detective*," she whispered back before wrapping her arms around his neck and kissing him.

Printed in Great Britain
by Amazon.co.uk, Ltd.,
Marston Gate.